IN YOUR EYES

J. KENNER

In Your Eyes

by

J. Kenner

Chapter One

"SEVEN WOMEN FROM MY SPIN CLASS," Taylor said, as she poured herself a glass of wine from the decanter on Megan's coffee table. "*Seven.* No, actually, wait, I forgot one. Eight. *Eight* of the women who took a flyer said that they're coming to the contest on Wednesday. Girlfriend, you're a genius. Either that, or Parker Manning is too gorgeous to be true."

"Why can't it be both?" Megan asked, feeling more than a little giddy at hearing how well her marketing idea had gone over. "I'm a certified promo guru, and Parker is sin personified. Because honestly, that man is a walking, talking orgasm. And you know what they say…"

"Sex sells?" Taylor asked.

"Abso-freaking-lutely."

The contest in question was the Man of the Month calendar contest, a bi-weekly event wherein local guys trotted across the stage—usually shirtless —to the applause and cheers of the bar patrons, most of whom tended to be female on contest nights.

So far, The Fix had crowned Mr. January all the way through to Mr. May, and the Mr. June contest was scheduled for Wednesday, just three short days away. Right before the last contest, Megan had come up with the idea of not only promoting the contest, but of promoting the men who were entering, the idea being that the entrants would share the fliers with friends and family to drum up more interest. And if any local celebrities were entered, that would start even more buzz.

Since the flyer had been her idea—and since she'd told two of her bosses, Tyree and Jenna, that they needed to ramp up the celebrity and sex appeal of the entrants—Megan had made it her mission to recruit guys into the contest who were well-known in the city or looked exceptionally hot without a shirt.

She was still working on convincing Matthew Herrington, a local gym owner, but she'd hit pay dirt with Parker Manning. The heir to a Texas oil fortune, Parker had the face of a movie star and the body of a Greek god. The kind of guy who looked like sex on a stick in jeans and a T-shirt, and sensuality personified in a suit or a tux. She'd never actually seen him shirtless, but she had no doubt that he would rock the world of every woman on the premises when he paraded across that stage come Wednesday.

Getting him had been a coup, but their overlapping history had undoubtedly helped. He'd been living in LA around the same time that Megan had been working as a make-up artist out there, and he'd run in the same circle as Carlton-the-prick and some of Megan's wealthier clients. They'd met a couple of times, and Parker had even asked her out once, but since she'd just started dating Carlton at the time, she'd turned him down.

When she learned that he'd moved back home to Austin—and, in fact, had bought a penthouse condo within walking distance of The Fix—Megan had known it was serendipity and had announced to her friends at the bar that she was going to recruit Parker Manning.

Everyone had been dubious. After all, Parker might be stunningly gorgeous with a reputation as a player, but he didn't seek out the spotlight. "I knew him in high school," Brooke Hamlin had told her. "And I just don't see it. Not because he's shy, but because he was always the guy who didn't have to put himself out there, you know?"

Actually, Megan did know. The Parker she'd known in LA exuded a cold, quiet confidence. As if he knew exactly who he was and didn't have any need to prove anything to anybody. A guy like that probably wouldn't want his face plastered on a bar flyer.

But then again, he was a local, and they did have a connection, and it wouldn't hurt to ask. So she had.

Not directly, of course. She'd approached him through his assistant, asking permission to use one of the pictures on Parker's Wikipedia page—a shot of him looking drop-dead gorgeous at a charity event. She'd also made sure that the assistant knew to mention to Parker that he'd known Megan in LA. She hadn't let herself get her hopes up, especially not after Brooke's revelation had supported her own assessment of the man, and so she'd been completely flabbergasted when he'd agreed within less than twenty-four hours.

The success had stoked her confidence, and

after a wild happy dance through her condo, she'd gotten back to work with a vengeance. Thanks to Parker, she'd lined up the rest of the men and had the flyers printed in record time.

"You have more flyers, right?" Taylor asked. "I'll take them to class in the morning and bring you the leftovers at the bar tomorrow night."

A graduate student in the drama department at the University of Texas, Taylor was not only a regular at The Fix on Sixth, she worked there on Wednesday nights when she stage-managed the actual contest.

"I do," Megan said, hopping up, then crossing to her desk—although it wasn't actually *her* desk since she was subletting the condo for six months, and getting a reduced rate since part of the deal involved pet-sitting two cats and three aquariums of exotic fish.

She'd ordered the first box of two hundred flyers three days ago, and already they were gone, picked up in various coffee shops, tacked to local bulletin boards, and circulated among the college sororities.

She hadn't expected them to go that fast, and so she'd gone back to the printer for two more boxes, one of which she now carried over to Taylor.

"Ta-da!" she said. "Plaster the town my friend."

Taylor took off the lid, and pressed her hand over Parker, who wore a tux and looked deliciously sexy in a James Bond sort of way. "Just give me a minute to soak up the awesome."

Megan rolled her eyes. "You know, the other guys aren't too shabby. I think we're probably giving them a complex." The flyer displayed the images of twelve hot men surrounding the logo for The Fix. Parker was only one-twelfth of the whole.

"Are you kidding?" Taylor shot back. "They're ridiculously excellent. If Parker wasn't in the mix, it would be a hard choice. But that boy's not only going to win, he's going to drive serious traffic to the bar. And then down the road he's going to sell a lot of calendars."

Since Megan couldn't disagree, she didn't. "Cheers to me," she said instead, clinking her glass with Taylor's before taking another sip.

"You know, if we're going to drink, we really should head to the bar. Mina's going to come down and meet us," she added.

Megan and Taylor had met at The Fix a few weeks after Megan had moved to Austin from Los Angeles, and they'd become good friends after they started running together while training for a 5K with the third in their trio, Mina.

"Mina may be coming tonight, but she's not coming for us." Mina's boyfriend, Cam, was covering for one of the weekend bartenders. "Besides," Megan added, "Griffin's going to walk over with us." She glanced at the time on her phone and frowned. "He should be here by now."

"All right, seriously. What's the deal with you two? I mean, you're totally sleeping together, right?"

"No!" Megan said. "We're just really good friends."

"Uh-huh," Taylor said, standing up and swinging her purse over her shoulder. "How about I head on to The Fix, and I'll meet you two there in a little bit."

"For crying out loud, Taylor. We're not dating. You don't have to leave us alone."

Taylor's head tilted to the side. "Does he know I'm here?"

"What? No. I don't know. Why?"

"Because that boy is super comfortable around you, but he doesn't really know me yet. And if he's meeting you here instead of at The Fix, don't you think that means he wants some chill time where he can just feel comfortable and not worry about what folks are thinking about his scars?"

"Why do people need to think anything about his scars?" Megan countered, though she knew the question was stupid. A childhood accident had left Griffin with massive scarring all over his right side. And though she didn't even notice anymore, she knew that outside of his family, she was unique in his life.

She'd told the truth about her and Griff; there was nothing romantic between them. But Taylor was also right. Megan and Griffin had clicked right away, and though they'd both thought that meant they should date, after one awkward kiss, they'd quickly realized they were more like brother and sister than boyfriend-girlfriend. So, yeah, Griff probably would like some down time with her before they joined the crowd.

With a sigh, she shrugged. "Okay, go ahead. We'll meet you there."

As soon as Taylor was out the door, Megan returned to the second story living area and peered out the window, watching her friend head toward Sixth Street even as she looked for the battered Mustang that Griffin was in the process of rebuilding.

Frowning when she didn't see it, she started to pull away from the window so she could grab her phone and send a text asking for an ETA. But the sight of a black car across the street made her pause. She hugged herself, warding off a sudden chill as she tried to chalk it up to the tank top she was wearing with her jeans. But it wasn't the outfit; it was that car. Had she seen it before? Had it been parked there yesterday?

A series of prickles raced up her spine, and she jumped a mile when the gate buzzer sounded. She clapped a hand over her chest, sighed, and told herself sternly to quit seeing ghosts where there weren't any. Los Angeles was behind her; nothing but a memory.

She had Austin now, a place she'd chosen on a whim that had turned out to be a brilliant inspiration. She loved this town, and she had yet to be disappointed. The food was great, the vibe was excellent, and she'd already surrounded herself with a fabulous circle of friends. Including the one who was at her gate at that very moment. And she was not going to screw it all up by worrying about shadows from the past. Carlton wasn't here. He wasn't coming here. And she needed to quit being paranoid.

After one more deep breath to steady herself, she trotted to the wall, then pressed the button for the intercom. "Griff?"

"You ready?" he asked from the pedestrian gate. "Or should I come in?"

"Come on in," she said as she hit the button to open the gate. "I still have to do my make-up." She didn't, however, intend to change clothes. Her jeans and Keep Austin Weird tank top might be ridiculously casual, but no one here would care. In LA, everyone had gotten dressed up for everything, but Austin was so much more laid-back. Besides, she still hadn't gotten used to the heat and the humidity, and tank tops had become her summer uniform of choice.

"Sorry I'm running late," she said when Griff reached her door. "Taylor came over for a while, but she cut out when I said you were on your way. Said she'd meet us at the bar."

"Yeah? Why didn't she stay?" he asked, pulling his hoodie off his head with one quick motion of his hand.

Megan gave herself a mental kick in the ass, because she wasn't about to admit to him that Taylor was being sensitive about his scars. "I'm pretty sure she thinks we're secretly dating."

"Quite the secret," he said, "considering neither of us is in on it."

Laughing, she hurried upstairs to finish getting ready. Which, considering they really weren't dating, didn't take that long. She put on light make-up, then pulled her hair up into a ponytail to keep the back of her neck from getting sweaty in the Austin heat.

"I'll have to tell Taylor that she can tell we're not dating by the fact that I'm wearing a tank top," she added when she returned to him.

"What? I'm not cool enough for you to dress up for?" he teased.

"This *town's* not cool enough to dress for. Honestly, maybe I'll hold off dating until fall," she added. "It's a wardrobe thing."

"A valid choice," he said. "I'm holding off until the next millennium. It's an ego thing."

"Griff…" She trailed off with a shake of her head. It was an argument they'd been having since almost the first day they'd met. "You don't need to be so self-conscious. We almost dated, and you weren't ever self-conscious around me."

"Yeah, but you're a make-up artist."

She paused at the door, baffled. "That doesn't

make sense. I'd think you'd be *more* self-conscious around me."

He shook his head. "No, you're trained to see past flaws. To you, enlarged pores are as much of a challenge as this mess." He indicated his face, only barely visible now that he'd pulled his inevitable hoodie back up. "Most people just see the surface and not the potential. If I date—"

"*When* you date," she corrected.

"When I date," he began again, "it'll be a woman who knows how to do that."

"Maybe you're not giving most women enough credit."

He shrugged. "Maybe not. Maybe that speech was an excuse to hide the fact that I'm just not ready."

Since that might actually be true, Megan decided not to press the point. But she hoped he found someone soon. Griff was funny and cool and talented. Between his work as a voice actor, his popular podcast, and the web series that had taken off like gangbusters, he was really making his mark.

But in the midst of all that attention, she feared that he was terribly lonely.

Still, push him too hard and she'd end up in the land of the hypocrite. Because her lack of interest in dating was about more than tank tops. She'd had a relationship in LA, and not a good one. Honestly, she wasn't inclined to repeat the experience anytime soon.

Still, that didn't mean she wanted to be celibate. Unlike Griff, she'd had a couple of hook-ups during her months in Austin. But that was more out of loneliness—or, if she were being honest—horniness. But those were just Band-Aids, not relationships. Not even close.

Heck, she didn't even do overnights. And the idea of opening her heart and soul to a man…? Well, she figured it would be a long time before she'd be ready to go down that road again.

Ready to go, they headed out of her unit and to the exterior gate. The Railyard Condos had been constructed from old warehouses in the downtown Austin area. And since the unit she'd sublet was near the west end of the property, they didn't have far to walk before they reached the intersection. They turned north, then continued the two blocks to Sixth Street.

"Oh, what the hell," she said, as much to fill the silence as to lighten her suddenly heavy mood. "Maybe we *should* just chuck it all and get married."

"Fair enough," he said as they turned left onto

Sixth Street. "If we're both still single by the time AARP starts sending us sign-up notices, we'll tie the knot."

"Deal." She caught his eye, and they both laughed, the heavy mood now gone. *Mission accomplished,* she thought as they approached The Fix on Sixth. Just being in the bar that she'd come to think of as a second home would have lifted her mood, but it was nice to go in smiling.

Considering it was past eight on a Sunday night, the place was surprisingly crowded, a fact that Griffin must have noticed, too, because he leaned toward her and said, "I think all the extra publicity is working. Double-edged sword, though."

She knew what he meant. The original owner of The Fix, Tyree Johnson, had been battling some financial issues recently. And he'd made it clear a few months ago that if The Fix was going to stay open past the end of the year, it needed to start showing a regular and solid profit.

More customers meant more profit, and that was a good thing, especially since the fate of the bar was at stake. But it also meant more people, even on nights when the place used to be mostly dead, and sometimes Megan feared that the bar would expand into something too crowded for comfort. A place where even if she could find a seat at the bar, once she sat down she'd realize that she didn't know anybody's name at all.

For now, at least, that was an idle worry. Not only did she and Griff both find seats at the far end of the long bar that ran parallel to the main wall, but the bartender, Cameron, brought over both of their usual drinks within seconds after they'd sat down. "Anything to eat?" he asked, his blue-gray eyes focusing on both of them in turn. "I know you guys love the Cobb Deviled Eggs."

A grad student at the University of Texas when he wasn't tending bar, Cam had also recently been promoted to Assistant Weekend Manager. Considering he'd never forgotten her drink and always recommended food that made her mouth water, Megan thought the promotion was well-deserved.

With his dark hair and broad shoulders, Cameron had recently earned the title of Mr. March in the upcoming Man of the Month calendar, and seeing him reminded Megan that she had a meeting soon with Eva Anderson, Tyree's fiancée and the official photographer for the calendar and the bar.

"Hey!" Taylor hurried over, flanked by Brooke Hamlin, a reality TV star who had pitched a show that focused on renovating the interior of The Fix. So far, they'd only been filming and editing, but the show was set to launch in August, and Megan anticipated that the crowds would grow once the show actually aired.

"Thank goodness you're here." Taylor slid in between Griff and Megan, but her attention was dead-on Megan. "Something's up. Something not good."

Megan frowned. "What are you talking about?"

"The flyer," Brooke said. "I overheard Jenna and Reece talking. But all I know is that there's some sort of crisis with the flyer."

"What? That's impossible." She looked down at the flyer she'd been so proud of and wondered what could possibly be wrong.

"It's probably nothing," Griffin said. She was sitting on his right side, as had become their habit, since she blocked his scars from strangers who might otherwise take a seat beside him. Now, he took her left hand in his right and squeezed, the scar tissue hard and tight against her skin.

"Don't worry," he said. "How bad can it be?"

Pretty bad, she realized less than three minutes later when Jenna hurried over. "I'm so glad you're here," Jenna said, relief and worry both lacing her voice. "I was about to call to see if you could come in. Tyree and I really need to talk to you. Like, now."

Megan glanced at Griffin who still looked clueless, but supportive. "Um, about what?"

"Parker Manning," Jenna said. "He saw the flyer, Megan. And he's pissed as hell."

Chapter Two

THE MOMENT she walked into Tyree's office, Megan knew what a condemned man facing a firing squad must feel like.

Tyree sat behind his desk, his hands clasped in front of him on his desktop and the light from the reading lamp making his dark skin gleam.

Jenna stood next to her fiancé, Reece, her ginger hair framing her face, her eyes focused somewhere over Megan's shoulder. Reece, the bar's general manager and co-owner, shot Megan a look of sympathy, which she would have appreciated more if she'd understood what the problem was.

It was Brent, the fourth owner and the bar's security guru, who actually spoke, his voice as gentle as if he was talking to his adorable five-year-old. "Thanks for coming in. Have a seat. I promise, we're not here to bite your head off, but we need to figure this out."

She continued to stand, then looked at each of them in turn, a horrible sense of foreboding welling in her gut. That, and disappointment. Because these people had given her a chance. Despite the fact that The Fix was trying to strengthen its financial position, they'd brought her on board without hesitation the moment that Jenna had heard that Megan was having a harder-than-anticipated time rebuilding her LA-based makeover business in Austin. She was ridiculously grateful, and she was terrified that somehow she'd screwed up—and screwed all of them by accident.

She drew a deep breath and forced herself to be calm. "I really want to make this right," she assured them. "But I don't even know what's going on? Why is Parker pissed?"

"Because of a mistake, we're sure," Tyree said, his gentle baritone filling the room. "But one that needs to be handled with care."

"Parker's got a lot of influence in this town," Reece added. "And if he decides to talk shit about The Fix, it won't be good for business."

Since that really didn't help, Megan shifted her attention to Jenna, who drew in a breath, then released it slowly. "I'm sure it wasn't your fault, Megan. But Parker called Tyree today and demanded that he be removed from the flyer and that The Fix issue a public apology."

Megan sat down with a thud. "What? But he can't do that. He agreed to participate. I gave his assistant all the details and he agreed."

Furious, she clutched the arms of her chair, afraid that otherwise she'd launch herself back to her feet and start reading Parker the Riot Act *in absentia*. Because this was bullshit. Seriously. The arrogant bastard. He thought that just because he had money and power he could pull the plug? He made a commitment, and dammit, he was going to stick to it.

She drew in a breath, forcing her temper down. This was a work issue, and no matter how absurd it was, she needed to handle it professionally. "If he's regretting his agreement, then I'm happy to speak with him. Or maybe it would be better coming from Reece and Tyree, since they've both been in the contest. He's made a fortune in the business world. Surely he understands that once he's given his word, there are repercussions for backing out."

"I'm sure he does understand that," Tyree said. "And I pointed out as much to him when we spoke.

But here's the problem—he assures me that he never signed a contract."

"Of course he did. I talked to his assistant, Lisa. And she called me back and said that he'd be happy to do it, and that she'd get the agreement over to me by the end of…"

She trailed off, her stomach going suddenly queasy as she realized that she never got the contract back. She put her hand to her mouth to ward off the rising bile.

"Oh, God," Megan said. "It is my fault. I totally screwed up big time."

MEGAN DRESSED in her lucky outfit on Monday morning, a black linen and silk blend tailored dress under a blazer with a timeless, classic cut. It was one of the outfits she'd splurged on in Los Angeles, determined to look like the professional she'd ultimately become.

It had cost her an entire month's profits, but it had been worth it, because she'd ended up making friends with Nancy, the Nordstrom tailor who'd done the alterations. Nancy had introduced her to Alice Gaines, the wife of a Los Angeles real estate developer whose friends included most of the rich and famous on both coasts. And within six months Megan had a steady stream of regular clients.

The dress had given her a career in LA. Maybe in Austin it could save her ass.

Because she wanted to look pulled together and professional, she accessorized with a string of pearls she'd inherited from her grandmother and the pearl earrings she'd bought for herself one Christmas.

She needed stockings to really complete the outfit, but pantyhose were out of the question in the July heat. And since thigh-highs invariably slid down her legs, she ended up wearing a garter and delicate nude stockings that she hoped she didn't run. Just in case, she tucked an extra one into her purse before sliding her feet into a pair of Chanel pumps with three inch heels that she'd scored at an online consignment store.

By eight-thirty she was out the door, and since the Austin office of PCM Enterprises was housed in One American Plaza, just a few blocks away from her condo, by eight forty-five she was standing in front of the reception desk, her heart pounding so hard it was a miracle the smiling gray-haired receptionist didn't offer to call the paramedics.

"I'm so sorry, Ms. Clark," she said as she ran

her finger down a printed list, "but I don't see you on Mr. Manning's appointment list. Let me just log in to his calendar and take a look. I'm sure—"

"No, that's okay," Megan said, her nerves finally settled enough so that she could form words. "I don't have an appointment. But I'm certain Mr. Manning will want to see me. There was an, um, misunderstanding about a project, and he spoke with my boss yesterday, and…"

She trailed off, realizing that she was rambling and that this woman didn't need the whole gory story.

"Anyway," she ended lamely. "I just need to see him."

"I'm very sorry, but Mr. Manning isn't in yet. I'd be happy to put you on his appointment list."

Leave and come back? Honestly, her nerves couldn't take it.

"Could I wait? Maybe he'll have time to squeeze me in before his first appointment."

"Well, I—" The woman met Megan's eyes, the corner of her mouth crinkling as she offered an understanding smile. "Certainly. Make yourself comfortable. Help yourself to coffee," she added, nodding at a machine on the far side of the reception area.

Since caffeine would just make her more jittery, Megan chose to sit and read a magazine. Or try to read. She wasn't really having much luck interpreting the little squiggles on the page as words. Instead, she looked around the room. At the perfectly decorated space. At the abstract art that suggested pills and powders, but was more decorative than informative.

Still, the art made sense considering PCM's core business was pharmaceuticals.

Other than the nature of his business, she knew only the basics about Parker Manning's background. Like the fact that his Houston-based family had money, that he'd boarded at a private high school in Austin, and that he'd moved to Los Angeles to go to college. According to various gossip sources, he'd dated actresses, dabbled in producing, and been front and center with two successful companies that he'd turned around and sold right after they hit big.

Rumor had it he'd tripled his net worth within a year, and the starting number had been none-too-shabby.

After that, he'd fallen a bit off the social media and tabloid radar, though there were still the occasional rumors about whom he was dating and where he was traveling. Then three years ago, he'd formed PCM Enterprises, a small pharmaceutical company that had rocketed to success, shifting Parker's image in the tabloids from useless, monied playboy to brilliant entrepreneur with a wild past, a shadowy present, and money to burn.

All of which had made him perfect for the Man of the Month contest, even though at the moment Megan was wishing she'd never heard of the man. And she was getting seriously tired of waiting to see him.

Antsy, she rose and crossed to the reception desk again. "Actually, maybe I could speak with his assistant first? Lisa."

"I'm sorry, Tracy Miles is Mr. Manning's current assistant, and I'm afraid she's out today."

"Oh." Well, great. So much for talking through what happened with the former assistant. She was probably fired for being an unorganized idiot.

Then again, Megan hadn't kept proper track either. If she had, she would have realized she'd never received the signed agreement back. As much as it sucked, this had been her project, her baby, and her stupid, lame-ass mistake.

What a mess. All she'd wanted to do was prove to the folks at The Fix that Jenna hadn't made a mistake in hiring her. That she actually had a brain and could help out with all of the various tasks at the popular bar. Most important, she'd wanted to pitch in with the marketing, because that was Jenna's area, and Jenna had taken a risk by offering Megan a job, even though The Fix was on a tight budget. And even though Megan knew buckets about makeup but next to nothing about marketing.

She'd spent two whole nights brainstorming ideas, and had been so proud when Jenna and Tyree had loved the idea of advertising the entrants in the Man of the Month contest on pre-contest flyers instead of simply promoting the winner after the fact. From that idea, it naturally flowed that they'd want to up the game a bit where the entrants were concerned.

Yes, most of the guys who'd been entering were total hotties, but very few of them were local celebrities. But if they could get some of the local television guys or wealthy business owners … basically anyone who made the news or the tabloids regularly, that would be a total plus. Especially if the guy was a social media draw.

And Parker Manning was about as social media centric as they came.

Megan had been foolishly certain that Parker

would participate, if for no other reason than that she was the one doing the asking. True, she'd turned him down when he asked her out, but that was only because of timing. The truth was, she'd been tempted. Yes, he'd had a bad boy reputation, but back in LA she'd been wilder and stupider, and there'd been a definite tug in the area of her nether regions.

She shivered. If she could take it all back, she would have dumped Carlton in a heartbeat and accepted Parker's invitation. If she had, maybe she'd never have seen Carlton again. Maybe she'd never have bolted.

She'd left Los Angeles without looking back, and her first sight of Parker in Austin had been an unpleasant twinge, especially since she'd been so careful not to reveal her location on social media or even contact any of her former clients for recommendations or referrals. Maybe she was being overly paranoid, but so be it. She'd left LA to get away from Carlton; she wasn't about to telegraph where she was.

She'd almost not approached Parker because of that. But she also recalled that the tabloids had reported on a rift between them, apparently a nasty one. And so she'd decided to take the risk. She'd remained a bit hesitant, though, and that was part of the reason why she hadn't asked him to participate personally, but had put the request out through his assistant, who'd told her he'd love to be part of it.

But apparently his former assistant was a space cadet—and Megan was an idiot.

Now Parker was pissed, and Megan had to somehow dig herself out of this hole.

She had no idea how she was going to manage that. She hoped their past acquaintance would smooth the way. And groveling was definitely on the menu.

"Ms. Clark?"

At the sound of her name, Megan jerked, her head snapping up as the magazine in her lap tumbled to the ground. Clumsily, she bent to retrieve it, then clutched it to her chest as she looked up at a tall, elegant woman standing just inside the frosted glass doors that led into the depths of the office. "Yes?" she squeaked.

"Mr. Manning will see you now. If you'll just follow me?"

She drew in a deep breath, then nodded as she fell in step behind the leggy blonde. Parker's office was down the hall. A corner office, of course, with a stunning view of the Capitol building, the University tower, and a wide spread of the Austin skyline.

More stunning than the view, though, was the man. Parker stood in front of his desk, leaning casually against it in a light gray suit that looked like it cost more than she made in a year. Possibly two.

His eyes met hers, an icy blue that somehow radiated heat, and she pushed her glasses more firmly up her nose, as if trying to lock him in focus.

"Ms. Clark," he said, his voice as cold as his eyes, but somehow underscored with a sensual tease. "I understand we have a little problem."

"I—well, yes." She tried to pull herself together, but dear God, he was distracting.

His eyes swept over her in an inspection so slow and intimate it left her with the distinct impression that he'd seen right through her simple black dress. "Fortunately, I have a solution."

"Oh," she said. "Um, what?"

That wide, gorgeous mouth curved up. "I thought that would be obvious, Megan. I want you."

Chapter Three

MEGAN BLINKED, certain she must have heard him wrong. "What did you say?"

Heat flashed in his eyes, and she swallowed, not certain if it was borne from anger or desire. "I think you heard me just fine."

"I—" She paused, her mouth dry and her words lost. She had no idea how to answer. For that matter, she wasn't sure how she felt. Was she confused? Insulted?

Was she, God forbid, actually a little bit flattered?

No. Absolutely not. He was being a prick and yanking her chain—and he was damn sure doing it on purpose.

She lifted her chin, determined to remain

professional even in the face of his antics. "I can't possibly have heard you right."

"No?" He pushed away from the desk and came toward her, and oh, holy hell, the man had a presence. He walked with purpose—and she couldn't shake the somewhat unnerving feeling that right then his purpose was her.

She shifted, intending to take a step back, but then she saw his lips twitch, and she was certain that he was laughing at her. Amusing himself by intimidating her, and patting himself on the back when it worked.

Bastard.

She dug in her heels and held her ground. "I came here to apologize for the misunderstanding and to ask you to please consider participating in the Man of the Month contest. The Fix on Sixth is a popular bar in a historic location on Sixth Street. This contest has turned into an incredibly well-attended event, and it's no secret that the contest is the cornerstone of a marketing campaign designed to increase revenue at the bar and, thus, keep it's doors open into next year and beyond."

Whew. She squared her shoulders and drew in a breath, impressed that she'd gotten all of that out without faltering. Then again, she'd practiced in front of her mirror for a good ninety minutes last night and once more on the walk over.

He cupped his chin in his fist, one finger extending onto his cheek as his head tilted slightly sideways. He looked like an academic—an insanely sexy academic. And she had absolutely no idea what he was thinking.

After a moment, he turned, walked behind his desk, and sat down, the city spread wide behind him. "Please," he said, with a nod to a leather and chrome guest chair.

She took the seat gratefully, certain that they'd passed the unpleasantries and were moving onto the details of how this would work and what The Fix could do to alleviate any inconvenience the whole mess had caused him.

Parker leaned back in his chair, his fingers now steepled under his chin. "Let me make sure I understand. You're telling me that—even though the error was entirely yours—because The Fix is a popular establishment with financial issues, I should enthusiastically tarnish my reputation and jump on board?"

She couldn't help it; her brows shot up. "Tarnish your reputation? *Yours*? The man whose picture's been flashed on the TMZ website more than Paris Hilton? *Your* reputation?"

He leaned forward, his hands clasped on his desk, his eyes on her, and his expression as commanding as she'd ever seen.

"Yes," he said, the easy tone belied by the formal posture. "*My* reputation. A reputation I've been working diligently to repair since I founded PCM Enterprises. A reputation that I've culled together piece by painful piece, meeting by interminable meeting with investors, doctors, FDA representatives, bankers, lobbyists, and more politicians than I like to think about. A reputation that I've clawed free from the wreckage of my bad choices in Los Angeles, and which you have just rendered invisible by including me in a line-up of men who are going to prance across a stage like a troop of goddamn Chippendale strippers."

"Oh." She licked her lips as she sank a bit into the chair. "Oh," she repeated, because she really didn't know what else to say.

With a rough shove, he stood, his chair rolling backward into the window from the force of his motion. For a moment, he simply stood there. Then he stalked around the desk until he was standing right in front of her, and she had to either tilt her head back to meet his eyes, or stay as she was with her eyes about level with his crotch.

She tilted, though the whole situation ticked her off. Dammit, she should have remained standing, because this position was intimidating as hell, and even though she'd screwed up, she'd come here to eat crow, *not* be intimidated. "I assure you, there is absolutely no prancing during the contest."

His brows rose. "Isn't there?" He stepped backward until he was leaning against his desk. "That's odd. Because I could have sworn the whole contest went something like this." He kept his eyes on her as he spoke, and all the while he was slipping off his jacket.

Her mouth went dry, and she actually jumped when he tossed it onto his desk. But she *really* almost lost it when he narrowed those ice blue eyes at her, loosened his tie, and then let it trail through his fingers as it dropped to the floor, as casually as a man undressing for bed.

During that whole process, he never stopped walking, and with each step closer her breathing grew more shallow and her body more aware. The man was like a sensual magnet, and the closer he came, the more her entire body seemed to yearn to go to him. Her blood humming. Her nipples peaking. Her lips tingling.

And then—oh, dear Lord in heaven—he started to unbutton his shirt. One button, then another, and another, until he paused right in front of her, the tiniest smattering of chest hair peeking out from the starched white cotton, so enticing that she almost had to sit on her hands to keep from reaching out to touch him.

He stopped after three buttons, and her mouth fell open, disappointment rolling off her in waves.

"Or am I wrong?" he asked, his voice low and very, very sensual.

It took her a second to remember her name, much less what they'd been talking about. "That wasn't prancing," she said, when her brain stared to function again. "It was preening."

Almost. He almost smiled at that. Instead, he managed to wipe his expression clear, then revealed nothing when he returned to the desk, once again leaned against it, and said, "I think you might be splitting hairs, Ms. Clark."

"I just mean that it *is* a calendar contest. Some amount of preening or prancing or strutting is expected." *And,* she thought, *he could strut for her anytime he wanted to.*

"Not by me. Since, as I already mentioned, I never intended to enter your contest. And by the way, did it even occur to you to ask my permission?"

Whatever sensual haze had started to descend on her, *that* completely obliterated it, and she almost leaped out of her chair. "Excuse me? Of course! I called and talked to your assistant. I specifically told her who I was, that I was calling on behalf of The Fix, and that we were hoping you'd participate in the contest."

"And then you just assumed I'd agree, so you went and plastered your flyers all over town."

"I—" She cut herself off. Dammit, she wanted to argue—to tell him that his previous assistant screwed up, which she had. But Megan had screwed up, too, and why get both of them in trouble?

"What?" Parker demanded as the silence lingered. "Did Lisa tell you she was sure I'd be happy to help, and you took that as gospel even before confirmation?"

"No," she lied. "No, I just asked for permission. And in my eagerness to get the flyer out, I guess I just assumed that you would do it."

For a moment, he said nothing. He simply watched her. When he finally spoke, all he said was, "Why?"

She shrugged, her frustration with herself rising anew. "Honestly, I don't know. Maybe because we used to know each other." She drew a breath and looked down at the floor. And then, because this was the time for *mea culpas*, she told him the rest of it. "Or maybe because once upon a time I thought that you liked me."

She lifted her eyes to look at him. "At least just a little."

He held her gaze, and his expression didn't change at all. But she thought she saw his shoulders sag just a bit. The silence between them grew thick until, finally, he said quietly. "I did. I do." The hint of a smile danced at the corner of his mouth. "Or maybe you missed the implications of my earlier negotiating point. I thought I'd made it clear that I want you."

She rolled her eyes. "That's not a reflection of like. That's a reflection of being an asshole."

"Careful — I can withdraw my very kind offer and watch you scramble to fix this mess you've tossed me into."

His words were intense, but his tone was light. So maybe they were reaching a detente?

She couldn't be certain, though. Just having her

in the room seemed to amuse him. And she couldn't risk screwing up again.

"I can fix this," she said firmly. "You say that I've damaged your reputation? We can use that reputation, and then walk away with it even stronger than before."

"I'm listening."

"Why don't we announce that you're doing it for a good cause. And for every vote for you, you'll donate $100 to charity."

He crossed his arms, looking both smug and amused. "So instead of you scrambling to fix this, I'm going write a very large check?"

"Um…"

"And what about all the men who don't win because I get the charity vote?"

She looked him up and down. "I just got a sneak peek at your prancing ability, remember? Believe me, you'll win even without the charity vote."

His brows rose, and she saw the flicker of heat in his eyes. But all he said was, "Nice try."

"Fine. You're right. It was a terrible idea." *Shit.* She was just digging herself in deeper and deeper.

"Actually, the charity idea's not bad. I can work with it."

"Really?" Relief positively flowed through her veins, as warm and sweet as hot fudge sauce. Thank goodness that was settled.

"Absolutely. We'll add it to the mix."

The rush of relief turned to icy slush. "The mix?"

He nodded. "You're clearly reluctant to accept my original proposal. Adding these few promotional benefits should make it worth your while. After all, turning the contest into a charitable fundraiser—even for one night—that's worth some media coverage for The Fix, I'm sure."

"Well, yes, but this conversation started because—"

She cut herself off. She couldn't actually remember how it had started, other than the fact that his initial compromise was to trade her for his participation in the contest. And that just wasn't happening.

"Look at me, Megan." His voice, commanding yet melodic, allowed for no disobedience, and the truth was that she was too tired and frustrated to fight him on the point anyway.

She looked up, and saw that the embers she'd seen in his eyes had flared into a burning desire so intense it sent a coil of heat curling all the way down to her core.

"The bottom line is that I want you, Megan. I wanted you in LA, and now here you are, all flustered and desperate. You've already knocked me back down to the man I was back then. A man used to getting whatever and whoever he wanted, including any woman who intrigued me, right there in my bed."

He took a step toward her, and her breath quickened. "And do you know why, Megan? It wasn't because of my bank account, though I'll admit that didn't hurt. No, it was because I have a certain skill set. I know where pleasure hides, and I know how to tease it out. I know how to tame desire and put a leash on passion. I have secrets, Megan. Secrets I can share with a woman—secrets that she'll beg for. Secrets that lead to treasures you can't even imagine."

Beads of sweat rose at the back of her neck. Sweat that had absolutely nothing to do with the sweltering temperature outside.

He bent forward, then pressed his lips close to her ear. So close the scent of him caressed her, a woodsy, male smell that would have seemed counter to the man in the business suit if she hadn't just witnessed the wildness inside. "Agree, Megan. You know you want to."

With supreme effort, she forced herself to shake her head. "No. What you're suggesting. It's … it's inappropriate."

He took a step back, stared at her for one long beat, then laughed.

"Yes, I suppose it is. And you can say no if you really want to. But I'm not the one who screwed up here, Megan." He took a step back, his hands threaded behind his neck as he looked at her. "We're done talking. It's time for you to make your choice."

She drew in a breath, her pulse pounding with anticipation. As if her body knew what the answer would be even before her brain got with the program. "Just one night, right? That's all?"

He nodded.

"And nothing I don't consent to?"

A single brow rose. "Well, dinner and a movie and a chaste kiss won't cut it." He let his gaze rake over her, from her head all the way to her toes, leaving her body tingling in the wake of his inspection.

"But don't worry," he said, when his eyes once

again met hers. "I don't do pain. Not unless you specifically ask for it," he added with a tiny smile.

She swallowed, wondering what the hell she was getting herself into, and more turned on that she cared to admit. Even to herself.

"No," he continued, bending over and putting his hands on the arms of her chair, essentially caging her in with his body. "I'm only interested in pleasing you, Megan. In making your heart pound and your skin fire. In tasting your lips, your breasts, every delicious part of you. Pleasure, remember? It's mine to give, and yours to enjoy. Come on, Megan. All you have to do is say yes."

She forced herself not to squirm in the chair, but she knew damn well that her panties were soaked. More than that, she was certain he knew it, too.

With a supreme force of will, she managed to not only look at him, but to conjure words. "If you want all that," she asked, "then why are you making it into a punishment."

He didn't answer. He only smiled.

And when the silence had lingered so long that she couldn't stand it, she waved the white flag and whispered, "Yes."

He nodded, just the tiniest movement of his

head. "Wednesday," he said. "We'll start our date after the contest is over. And take Thursday off from work. We don't want to rush things, after all."

Her eyes went wide, and he chuckled. "Thanks for coming in today, Ms. Clark. It's been a pleasure doing business with you."

———

HE WAS AN ASSHOLE.

A first-rate, A-number-one, certifiable asshole.

But at least he knew it, so maybe that went part of the way toward redeeming him.

Parker didn't know. Frankly, he didn't care. Not so long as he got what he wanted.

And what he wanted was Megan.

With a sigh, he settled in the guest chair she'd vacated, still warm from her body. Her perfume lingered along with her heat—a vanilla essence that tickled his senses. He had a weakness for white cake with vanilla cream frosting, but at the moment, he was craving something even sweeter.

But not just sweet. Strong, too. And his cock tightened with anticipation and desire as he pictured her sitting right in that chair and owning up to her mistake.

For a moment, he simply enjoyed the memory. But then he levered himself out of the chair and circled his desk. Frowning, he pushed the button on his phone to call the reception desk, then waiting until Mrs. Ridley's efficient voice came on the line.

"Yes, Mr. Manning?"

"Is Lisa in?" She'd been his assistant for less than three months, but her lack of attention to detail had sealed her demise. Rather than fire her, though, he'd had Human Resources relocate her. Now, he believed, she worked as a file clerk.

"She is, sir. Shall I send her up?"

"Please." He ended the call, then waited, not entirely certain what had possessed him to go down this particular road. After all, Megan had been perfectly clear that she'd jumped the gun in printing the flyers, and that Lisa had never suggested that he was willing to participate.

Even so, he wanted to talk to the girl himself.

She arrived within five minutes, then wiped what were undoubtedly sweaty palms on her slacks. The girl got nervous and flustered if you so much as looked at her wrong. Yet another reason she wasn't assistant material. He needed an assistant who anticipated him, not one who jumped every time he spoke to her.

"You're not in trouble," he said, because that was the best way to begin every conversation with her. "I'm trying to clear up a misunderstanding and just need to get a few details."

"Oh." She blinked. "Okay. Sure."

"I understand that you told someone at The Fix that I'd participate in their Man of the Month contest." He actually didn't understand that at all. In fact, he assumed the opposite. Hell, Megan had confirmed that Lisa hadn't pulled such a bone-headed maneuver as signing him up for an event without first clearing it with him.

All he wanted was for her to deny it.

Instead, she nodded. "That's right. It's a very popular event. I went with my friends after work about a month ago. We saw Mr. April. That radio guy won. The DJ who's so funny during the morning show when—"

"Lisa."

She closed her mouth, her eyes open wide.

"Is there a reason you never told me about it?"

Miraculously, her eyes opened even wider. "Oh, no, sir. No reason at all."

He considered responding, thought better of it, then nodded. "Thank you, Lisa. That's all I needed to know."

"Oh. So I can go?"

"You can go. Thanks."

He pressed his fingers to his temples, fighting a headache that was creeping in.

At least he'd confirmed that he'd made the right decision by transferring Lisa off his desk.

And at least he'd confirmed his suspicions that Megan had taken it on the chin, purposefully covering for his assistant's ineptitude.

With a sigh, he looked out the window, thinking.

The truth was, he'd been intrigued by Megan from the first moment he'd met her, but she'd ended up in Carlton's arms before Parker had made a move. He was shallow enough to admit that it was her looks that had initially caught his attention. Her long, glorious hair, so dark against her fair skin. Those big brown eyes that today had been hidden by teal-rimmed glasses. Her slim body and subtle curves. And that sweet, sweet smile that had the power to shatter him.

He'd wanted to mold her against his body and twine his fingers in her hair. He wanted to lose himself in the depths of those eyes and bask in the glory of her smile.

But while her looks had fascinated him, her personality had intrigued him. He'd always had a weakness for ballsy women, and she certainly qualified. After all, he knew she'd moved to LA without a dime. And she was fiercely self-reliant, too. That much she'd proven today when she'd refused to blow the whistle on Lisa.

He'd thought he'd lost her when she'd unexpectedly left LA without a word to anyone, but after he moved the corporate offices of PCM to Austin three months ago, he'd seen her on the street and realized that she'd moved here, too.

As far as Parker was concerned, that was one hell of a Cosmic sign.

Between the coincidence of Austin and Lisa's screw up, it was clear that Fate was giving him another chance—one he didn't intend to fumble.

And that somehow, someway, he'd have Megan Clark in his arms ... and in his bed.

Chapter Four

WEDNESDAY NIGHT ARRIVED both ridiculously fast and interminably slow. Monday had been a haze, Tuesday a whirlwind, and today a slow grind. The only real break had come a few hours earlier when Beverly Martin—a rising indie star who'd agreed to be the contest emcee—had arrived at Megan's condo for a makeup session.

"You've met the full line-up, right?" Bev had asked. "Who do you think will win?"

Parker. It was a no-brainer as far as Megan was concerned. Aloud, she'd said, "I'm really not sure."

"Mmmm." Bev's tone had suggested fine chocolate or finer sex. "My money's on Parker. We met when I was in LA after *Suburban Love Song* got nominated." She flashed the kind of smile that suggested she had a sexy secret. "That man is definitely calendar worthy."

"Definitely," Megan had said brightly, but her insides had done an unpleasant twisting thing as she wondered if Bev and Parker had gone out. Not that it mattered to her, of course. Really.

Non-existent jealousy aside, doing Bev's makeup had been a nice reprieve from the constant nerves and worries about this evening with Parker, but Bev had been gone for over an hour now, and Megan's nerves had shifted back into high gear.

At least it was finally time for her to get dressed and head to The Fix for tonight's contest.

And for all the things that would come after.

Her stomach flipped over as a fresh wave of jitters overwhelmed her. Sternly, she told herself to chill, and she was coming close to managing that when another thought occurred to her—*Thursday.*

Parker had told her to take off Thursday, and she'd done so, confirming the time off with Tyree and Jenna as soon as she'd arrived at The Fix on Monday after her meeting with Parker.

Then, of course, she'd done her best not to think about the implications. Because, well, *whoa.* She'd anticipated a very late night on Wednesday, with the possibility of another round of—well, *what-*

ever—on Thursday morning. But the whole day? Why did she have to take off the entire day?

She'd decided not to worry about it. But now that Wednesday was here and Thursday was fast approaching, she couldn't avoid the issue.

Was he yanking her chain?

Or maybe he was just determined to get a full twenty-four hours? That was certainly possible. After all, because of the contest, their date couldn't even really get started until nine-thirty.

But he'd said he wanted her, and she knew that didn't mean coffee and chitchat. So maybe he really was anticipating some sort of overnight sexcapade? A wildly sensual affair in a premium hotel with the kind of all-night activities that she was certain Parker was expert at—and which were designed to make a woman melt.

She swallowed, her mouth suddenly dry. *Did she want that?*

Her mind very primly announced that she most certainly did not.

But if the way her skin was tingling was any indication, her body had a very different opinion.

Frustrated, she grabbed her hairbrush off her dresser, then stood at the window brushing out the knots as she looked idly out the window, her mind on tonight as she pondered the myriad of possible activities Parker might have in mind.

Honestly, it could be anything.

Anything.

A shiver cut through her and she hugged herself as she realized just how true that was. Parker had been friends with Carlton, after all. Who knew what proclivities he might have?

Frustrated, she tilted her head, then began to brush more vigorously. She was being paranoid and unfair. Carlton never actually hurt her, and he'd never done anything overly kinky. He'd just gotten a little weird.

Still…

Parker might turn out to be weird, too. Had she leaped from the frying pan into the fire?

She didn't think so. He felt … well, *right*. Arrogant and demanding, yes. But not in a way that made her skin prickle with apprehension. On the contrary, the only tingles she'd felt around Parker were sparks of anticipation.

And that was an entirely different kind of danger.

She drew a deep breath, then started to step away from the window.

That's when she noticed the car. Sleek and

black, just like the one she'd seen from her window on Sunday. And, once again, it was double-parked right across the street from her condo, the interior light indicating that someone was sitting inside.

With a shiver, she pulled her robe tight around her, trying to ward off a sudden chill. No such luck, mostly because the room was warm and the chill was in her blood, a bone-deep shiver that she wouldn't be able to quench with a down-filled mountaineering jacket, much less the thin robe she'd picked up on sale at Target.

She forced herself to step away from the window. Because this was nothing. No big deal. Just one black car on the street below her bedroom window. There was no reason to think it was a menace to her or anyone else. Maybe it was looking for parking. Maybe it was marking time until one of the other residents hurried to meet their ride. There were a million possible reasons why a car would be on a street, and most every one of them was innocent.

Besides, there was no way to know if she'd actually seen *this* particular car before. Heck, it probably wasn't even the same model she'd noticed on Sunday. And even if it was, so what? A slew of people lived in The Railyard condos; there was no reason to think the car had any connection to her, right? *Right.*

Annoyed by her lingering fears, she moved back to the window. All clear. Not a black car in sight.

Her shoulders sagged with relief, reassured that Carlton hadn't somehow found her. That he hadn't come all the way from Los Angeles to Austin just to mess with her.

Honestly, she was being ridiculous. She'd been in Austin for over three months now, and she hadn't heard a peep from him. It was over. It was done. She'd moved on.

Moved? Try *ran.* And, yes, maybe that had been an over-reaction, but as far as Megan was concerned, better safe than sorry. Her sister, Leslie, had waited too long to get away from Jerry, and while Megan was relieved that Leslie had come out okay in the end, she had no desire to repeat her sister's mistakes.

And, no, maybe Carlton's weirdness wasn't really pointing that way, but there'd been signs. She could have overlooked the increase possessiveness while they were dating, labeling it as a protective streak. But it was after she'd broken it off with him, that she'd started to get twitchy. The late night calls from blocked phone numbers. The cars that parked outside her apartment. Flowers delivered with sensual notes and no signature. And that horrible, persistent sensation of being watched.

So she'd cut and run. Left LA for Austin, a town to which she'd had no prior connection, so why would anyone look for her there? A town with enough wealth and entertainment types to ensure that a freelance make-up artist could squeeze out a living.

Except it turned out that *squeezing out a living* thing was harder than it sounded, not in small part because Austin was freaking expensive.

Thank goodness for The Fix.

She drew in a breath, her circular thoughts finally coming to rest on what was really important at the moment—getting dressed and getting to the club.

With one final frown toward the window, she pulled on the yellow sundress with the fitted bodice she'd picked out for tonight. Simple and flattering, and she paired it with jeweled sandals and a thin cotton sweater. It was the most versatile thing in her wardrobe. Casual enough to wear to The Fix and flirty enough to pass if Parker took her somewhere nice for dinner. And since Parker hadn't given her a clue what to wear, it was just going to have to do.

She didn't see any sinister vehicles during her short walk to The Fix, but even so, she was thrilled when she stepped inside the bar and saw Griffin waving her over.

"You look nice. What happened to the usual jeans and *The Fix* T-shirt for contest night?"

"Just changing things up," she said, not quite meeting his eyes.

"Mmm." He signaled Eric to bring him a fresh drink, then ordered her a water since she was technically on the clock until the contest wrapped. "I saw that Parker Manning's still on the contest line up," he added. "How'd you convince him?"

"Oh, we're turning his participation into a whole charity thing. You'll hear about it when Bev does the intros."

"Uh-huh," he said, once again looking at her outfit. This time when he met her eyes, there was a knowing look in his. "Christ, Megan, you didn't—"

Thankfully, she was saved by the exuberant arrival of Amanda Franklin, a local real estate agent and a regular at The Fix. She was also one of Jenna's best friends, and that connection had spilled over onto Megan.

"Amanda!" Megan gave her a friendly hug, a little more exuberant than necessary, but she was so grateful that Amanda's arrival had waylaid Griffin's questions.

"Hey, girl! Jenna told me everything you've done—"

Megan rolled her eyes at that, making Amanda laugh.

"Yeah, she told me everything," she admitted, with emphasis on *everything*. "But she also said that you fixed it. So good job."

Amanda glanced around the crowded bar, that was becoming more crowded by the second. "You know, I think this may be the best night yet. Your flyers definitely upped the interest, and what's on the flyer's not too bad either. I mean, Parker? Holy hell, that man is hot."

Griff rolled his eyes, but Megan just laughed. "Seriously hot," she admitted, enjoying the nice warm buzz of her secret. He *was* hot. And tonight, he was her date. Assuming she could stretch the definition of *date*, that is.

"Honestly, if this were a bachelor auction instead of a calendar contest, I think I'd have to bid." Amanda started to fan herself, and Megan had to clap a hand over her mouth to keep from laughing, because Parker had come up right behind her, and even with the din, there was no way he could have not heard her.

"Hey," he said, his attention focused entirely on Megan. "I'm looking forward to tonight."

In front of him, Amanda twisted to look behind her, her eyes going wide when she saw him, then widening even more when she caught sight of his companion, a man with short dark hair, pale gray eyes that looked like they hid a thousand secrets, and a wide mouth that was curved into the slightest hint of a smile.

Megan was about to ask who the man was, but Griff spoke first, his words directed to Parker. "You said you're looking forward to tonight?" The question sounded like an interrogation. "You mean the contest, right?"

"Of course," Parker said, though he was looking at Megan and not Griffin. "What else?"

Griffin didn't answer, and Megan didn't look at him. But she could feel his gaze boring laser-like into her skull. "Who's your friend?" she asked Parker, mostly as a diversionary tactic, but also because she was genuinely curious.

"Sorry," Parker said. "Everyone, this is Derek Winston."

They all introduced themselves, shaking hands

in turn. Perfectly normal, except that Megan noticed that Amanda hesitated, then pulled her hand free a tad too early. An odd reaction considering Amanda was the last person Megan would expect to be intimidated by a good-looking guy.

"You're Winston Hotels, right?" Griffin asked, the question shifting Megan's attention from Amanda and back to Derek. "Nice properties."

"Thanks," Derek says. "It's a family business, but I've taken over as the director of North American operations. I'm in town for personal visits to the three Austin properties. Since Parker and I go way back, I thought I'd come watch him shake his groove thing up on that stage."

"If my groove thing does any shaking—" Parker glanced so swiftly at Megan that it might have been her imagination, "—it won't be on that stage."

"There you are!" Taylor's familiar voice fell over their group, and then the woman herself shoved her way through the crowd, saving Megan from another round of questions from Griffin.

Taylor grabbed Parker's arm, and a jealous soup started to boil in Megan's gut, even though she knew perfectly well that the gesture wasn't intimate. Taylor was the contest's stage manager, and the hardest part of her job was wrangling the contestants to their places back stage.

Not to mention the fact that Megan could hardly feel jealous about a man she had no claim over in the first place.

"See you all later," Parker said, speaking to all of them, but his attention on Megan.

"Good luck," she called. She expected Amanda to say the same thing, but she was focused on her phone, though Megan had the distinct impression that the device was a prop, and Amanda was really in massive avoidance mode.

But who—or what—was she avoiding?

That, however wasn't something she could think about at the moment. "I need to go check on Beverly," she said, pointing to the emcee, who was signaling for Megan to come to the stage. "Nice to meet you, Derek," she said before hurrying toward the stage with Griffin at her side.

"You want to tell me what's going on with you and Parker?"

"No," she said simply, to which his eyes widened. She paused long enough to draw a deep breath. "I mean yes, but later. Drinks tomorrow night?"

He looked like he wanted to argue, but he

nodded. "Fine. I'll go grab us some seats at the bar. You do your thing and meet me there."

She nodded, then hurried over to Beverly, passing Taylor on her way back. "I swear it's like herding cats," the stage manager said, making Megan laugh.

"You're in a good mood," Beverly said, as Megan did a quick touch-up on her make-up. The show was being filmed so that segments of the contest could be edited into *The Business* Plan, the reality TV show that centered on the remodeling of The Fix. Because of that, Megan knew that Beverly was hyper-conscious of her appearance on that stage. Not that she had reason to be. Bev hit all corners of the celebrity triangle as far as Megan was concerned. Natural beauty, genuine niceness, and natural talent.

"Perfect," Megan said. "Now go."

"Thanks," Beverly said. "Time to break a leg."

Megan laughed, then turned to head back toward the bar and Griffin. She didn't make it, however, because she caught sight of Jenna and Reece standing at the edge of the stage.

"Hey," Jenna said, waving her over. A wide grin lit her eyes as Megan approached. "Good job turning a screw-up into a victory."

"Thanks. I won't deny it was stressful."

"But you pulled it off," Reece said. "Congratulations."

He had his arm around Jenna, who was leaning against his broad chest, looking a little tired.

"You okay?"

"Oh, yeah. Fine," Jenna said. "Just wiped."

"Do you want me to grab you a chair?" Megan asked. She was certain that Jenna was pregnant, but she and Reece had still not officially said anything to their friends.

"I've got one for her right here," Reece said, pointing to the chair that his large body was blocking. "She says she won't have a view." He rolled his eyes, then flashed a mischievous grin. "What's she need to see these a-holes for? She's already got me."

"And I'm keeping you," Jenna said, then winked at Megan. "Doesn't mean I can't window shop."

Megan bit back a smile, her attention turning to Reece. They'd actually shared a one-night stand a few months back, before he and Jenna had gotten together. Megan had just arrived in Austin and had been feeling lost and lonely. Reece had felt the same. She'd been running from a man, and he'd been running from his desire for a woman he didn't think he could ever have.

Reece had gotten his happily ever after, and though Megan would never begrudge him that, she couldn't deny the envy that curled through her as she looked at him and Jenna together.

Reece was living his dream, lost in love and family.

And Megan? She was off to have one more shallow encounter with a man who made her pulse pound, but who she knew didn't really want her. All he wanted was payment.

She tried to tell herself that was okay. She was young. Why shouldn't she go out? Have fun? Have sex?

There was nothing wrong with that, not so long as she was careful and smart.

And maybe that was true.

But it wasn't a question of wrong or right.

It was a question of *more*. She wanted more than a one night stand. More than a fast fuck, even with a gorgeous man with exceptional skill.

She wanted the full meal deal, and she wanted it super-sized.

But she was starting to be afraid that she was never going to actually find it.

"Megan?"

She jerked up, twisting around to find Jenna looking at her. "You look lost."

"Sorry. Mind wandering."

Thankfully, the theme music started up, and she didn't have to say more. Instead, she rose up on her tiptoes and craned her neck over the crowd so that she could see the back of the room where Parker and the other men gathered in the doorway to the back bar waiting on their cue.

As if he sensed her attention, Parker looked up, his eyes meeting hers, full of heat and promise. Slowly, he smiled, and she sighed with pleasure as the heat of that smile warmed her soul.

Maybe she didn't have what Reece and Jenna had. Maybe she never would.

But for tonight, at least, she had Parker.

And Megan would take what she could get.

Chapter Five

"–TO BEGIN!" Beverly chirped, her bright smile lighting up the room. She held up her hands, and Megan had to smile at how expertly she settled the crowd. "But before we get going, I have a quick announcement. Those of you familiar with the Man of the Month contest will notice that tonight's contest is a little different. Thanks to the kind suggestion of contestant Parker Manning, tonight's contest not only benefits all you women in the audience—"

"And gay men!" someone yelled from the back, causing the room to erupt with laughter.

Beverly laughed, too, but didn't lose her stride, "—it also benefits the favorite charities of each of the contestants. And, of course, you are all supporting our favorite local bar, The Fix On Sixth, by coming here tonight, buying the drinks, and eating the food."

She went on to explain that Parker was donating one-hundred dollars per vote to each contestant's favorite charity. As for the winner, he was taking that number and multiplying it by ten. But in order to make sure that the votes were for the men and not the charities, the guys wouldn't announce their selected charity until after the competition.

"And that's it," Beverly said, wrapping up as the contest music started. "Let's give a warm welcome to our first contestant, Parker Manning!"

The room erupted, and Megan lifted herself onto her tiptoes, trying to see over the taller heads in front of her as Parker sauntered up the red carpet waving at the audience and generally soaking up the appreciation.

And, just as he'd done in his office, with each step he took, more of his outerwear came off. First the tie, which he flung into the audience. Then he unfastened the buttons. One, then another, then another. All the way down until his shirt was hanging completely open by the time he reached the stairs to climb up onto the stage.

Megan stood to the left of the stage, and now

that he'd come closer, she had a clear view. First of his chest, broad and firm with a perfect six pack and deep cuts that angled down from his hips and led under his tight, faded jeans. Jeans that, she noticed, he'd unbuttoned. Not to reveal anything, but just to give that extra edge of heat.

Everyone on that side of the stage could see his picture-perfect body, and when he took the next step and peeled the shirt all of the way off, she heard gasps from the women behind him, and a sharp jolt of envy cut through her that *she* didn't have a view of his broad shoulders and tightly muscled back.

What she *did* have was his attention. Because he'd paused on the steps leading up to the stage, and his eyes were fixed on hers, so intently that Megan wasn't entirely sure if she could recite her own name, much less tell anyone what city she was in. All rational thought had been replaced by one basic truth.

Mine.

Tonight, she thought, *he's mine.*

Then a voice shrieked from her left— "Oh, yeah, baby! Come to momma!" —and Parker turned that direction, twirled the shirt once over his head and sent it flying toward the shrieker.

What the hell?

Megan's mouth fell open, and the cold hard claws of jealousy cut right through her. He should have tossed that shirt to *her*.

His eyes found hers, and she saw the fire of victory there. And she knew in that moment that he'd tossed the shirt away on purpose—and that he'd know damn well it would light a fire under her lust.

Busted.

He finished climbing the steps, walked the length of the stage, and flexed his muscles for a gaggle of screaming women.

Then he stepped back out of the light as one by one the other eleven men joined him on stage. But Parker was a hard act to follow, and as far as Megan was concerned, they'd all lost the competition even before it started.

The men left the stage as the votes were being tallied, and Megan was more relieved than she ought to be when Parker only politely nodded to the women who grabbed at him as he walked by, their greedy fingers brushing his bare skin.

He didn't hesitate, didn't pause. Instead, he moved straight to her side and put his hand on her waist, pulling her close so that she had no choice but to brush against his hot, naked skin. *Oh. My.*

"Miss me?" His words were a whisper, his breath caressing her ear, and she felt the tremor of contact rush all the way down her spine.

Yes. But she was hardly going to admit it. Instead, she purposefully took a step out of his embrace so that she could see him better. Then she lifted her brows and tried to look down her nose at him. Tricky, since he was a full head taller than she was. "Why would I miss you? You were only a few feet away."

He didn't argue, but his smug smile told her that he knew she was full of shit.

Well, fine. This was supposed to be their wild sensual encounter, wasn't it? And considering she was the envy of every woman in that room, she damn sure intended to enjoy it.

"*Heads-up.*" Griffin's call came from a few feet away, and when Megan looked that direction, she saw a black T-shirt flying through the air.

Parker caught it with one hand, then smiled down at her. "What do you say? Should I put it on?"

"You'll disappoint every woman in this bar."

"Including you?"

She hesitated, then decided to go for the gold and tell him the truth. "No."

Surprise flickered in his eyes. "Why not?"

She drew in a deep breath for courage. "I'm supposed to be yours tonight, right?"

A slow, easy smile slid across his face. "I thought I was clear," he replied in a voice as smooth and rich as fine whiskey. "There's no *supposed to be* about it. Tonight, you *are* mine."

"And that means you're mine, too." She lifted her chin. "And I don't like to share."

For the length of a heartbeat, he said nothing. He simply met her eyes and held her gaze. Eternity lingered in that moment, full of a violent heat that swirled around her, making her a little dizzy, but also filling her with a potent anticipation.

"Fair enough," he finally said, as he held up the shirt. She watched the play of his muscles as he pulled it on, then drew in a sharp breath when his head emerged and his attention was once again fully on her.

"Let's get out of here." His voice was low and full of purpose, and with every breath in her body she wanted to say, "Yes."

Instead, she said, "We have to wait for the tally." Of course, that wasn't entirely true. The staff at

The Fix encouraged the contestants to stay. But there'd been a couple of times when the contestants —even the winners—had scattered before the announcement. So long as they came back for the calendar shoot, it was all good. The party in the bar would still go on.

"If we leave now, I'll add an extra zero to all twelve donations."

She swallowed. "That's not exactly sound money management."

"On the contrary, I'm using my money to buy myself something I truly value, support twelve excellent causes, and incur significant tax deductions. Sounds like a win all around to me." He lifted his hand, signaling to Jenna, who was talking with Beverly.

Both women came over, and though it was clear that Jenna was about to say something, he cut her off with one quick motion. "I'm afraid I have to go deal with a crisis, and I need to head out."

"Oh. But Taylor said the results will be tallied any second."

Megan leaned forward, intending to say that he could certainly stay for a few more minutes, then shocked herself by explaining his plan to add an extra zero to every donation. "It's a shame he has to run," she concluded. "But it's such a generous offer. And think of the positive press coverage for The Fix that will go along with it."

She nodded at the two other women, who looked at each other, both appearing slightly baffled.

"I appreciate your understanding," Parker said to them, then added, "Ms. Clark? I believe my car's waiting on the street. Walk with me?"

Megan shot Jenna what she hoped was a *what can you do* expression, then hurried to match Parker's stride as she fought an almost overwhelming urge to giggle.

As he'd predicted, a car was waiting for him on the street. "When did you manage to send a text to your driver?"

His slow smile sizzled. "I'm a man of many talents."

"I'll just bet you are."

A shock of awareness cut through her when he put his hand on her lower back, then led her to the car. Before they could get in, though, Griffin called to them from the doorway of The Fix. "Manning! Hey, Manning."

Parker turned, Megan at his side.

Griffin strode over, his eyes fierce. "What kind

of game are you playing? And don't even think of bullshitting me."

"Nothing Megan hasn't agreed to."

"Griff, please…"

For a second, Griff said nothing, and Megan actually feared he was going to make a scene or ask Parker his intentions or insist on coming along as a chaperone.

Instead, he cocked his head and said, very slowly and clearly, "If I learn that you hurt her in anyway—one tear, one pricked finger, one bruised ego—I will ride your ass so hard you'll swear I was a hemorrhoid."

"Not loving the imagery," Parker said. "But I get the message. And you have my word."

Griff met Megan's eyes, and she silently pleaded with him to please, please just go back into the bar.

Thankfully—miraculously—he did.

Parker watched him go, and when he turned back to face Megan, she was surprised at the expression on his face. Not irritation, but something warm and friendly. Something like approval.

"You have a good friend in him," Parker said once they were both in the backseat. "Or is he more than a friend?"

"No," she admitted. "We'd thought maybe ... but no."

"Good." Parker's gaze locked on hers, his words both confusing and pleasing her. She had no idea how she'd gone from completely screwing up the flyer to being the recipient of such heated glances and sensual awareness, but she wasn't going to complain.

But at the same time...

She tilted her head, studying his face, and he looked back at her, amused.

"What?"

"It's just ... well, why *good*?"

His brows rose with obvious confusion.

"I only mean that if this is a one night thing, what does it matter if there's something between me and Griffin?"

"Distractions." He turned slightly in the seat so that he was looking at her directly. Then he took her hand, his thumb gently stroking her palm as his low, melodic voice caressed her senses. "We've been talking in circles, so let me be clear. I intend to take you to sensual heights that you haven't imagined. To bring you such pleasure you beg me to stop, then scream my name in protest when I do."

Anticipation rippled through her, leaving her

aching and breathless, but he didn't even pause in his relentless seduction.

"I'm going to hold you close while you shatter, and then I will slowly and deliberately, put you back together again."

He moved his hand onto her thigh, this new delight making her gasp. His palm rested on the material of her dress, but his fingertip brushed her bare leg, and it seemed that the point of contact was all that she knew, all that she was. He was driving her crazy with that innocent touch coupled with his delicious promises, and yet he didn't even acknowledge the state into which he'd already led her.

"That's my mission, Megan. And I intend to pursue it relentlessly." The fingertip stopped its erotic ministrations. "Do you understand?"

She wasn't sure she did. All she knew was that he'd intoxicated her with his words. But she nodded anyway. A little overwhelmed, a little numbed.

"Pleasure is as much a mental response as a physical one. Do you think you'd feel as much from my touch if you were thinking of another man?"

She swallowed, unable to imagine how any other guy could possibly squeeze into her thoughts past the force of nature that was Parker Manning.

"Do you remember what I said in my office?" he asked, then continued before her spinning thoughts could conjure an answer. "I want you, Megan. Body and mind. I want your submission. Your trust. Your surrender. Most of all, I want to please you. I want you to go as far as you can, and I want to be the one to take you there."

For the first time, she realized that he'd been easing the hem of her dress up as he spoke. Now his fingertip grazed her inner thigh, just mere inches from her now-damp panties, and suddenly that point of contact seemed like all she knew in the world.

"Do you understand?"

She nodded, not trusting her ability to form words.

"Good, then come on."

With a start, she realized that the car had stopped moving. More than that, they appeared to be on a tarmac, parked a few yards from a small jet.

She turned to him. "Go as far as I can?" she said, referring to his earlier words. "Is this what you meant? A trip?"

"No," he assured her as he twined his fingers with hers. "But it's a start."

Chapter Six

MEGAN STOOD beside him on the tarmac, her eyes fixed on the jet, and Parker felt his stomach sink. In the car, she'd been responsive. Open to his touch. He'd seen the surrender in her eyes when he'd told her that he wanted her. He'd watched her skin glow as the heat of a blush warmed her skin when he promised her pleasure.

His fingertip still tingled from heat of her skin against his, and his entire body ached with a need that had been building since the moment she walked into the bar wearing that flirty dress with the fitted bodice, its tiny white buttons practically begging to be ripped open.

They should have kept driving. Hell, they should have gone to a fucking Denny's. Anything to have kept the look of growing passion in her eyes, and to have shut out this expression of apprehension he saw creeping onto her face.

All night, he'd craved the moments when he could be alone with her. In the car. On the jet. Long moments when it was just the two of them with a drink, a caress. With words and lips and decadent promises.

Now, though, he was afraid that Desire had made him her bitch, and that by bringing Megan here, he'd pushed her too far.

The irony was that he never used his money as an enticement for women. He never took them to his penthouse. Never flew them to exotic locations. Never zipped across town in his Ferrari or took them out for a Saturday afternoon shopping spree, filling their closets with jewelry and designer clothes.

When he was younger, he hadn't wanted to spend a dime of his father's money on himself or anyone else. And now that he had his own money, he only wanted to use it when it mattered.

Tonight, it had mattered. *She'd* mattered.

But he hadn't factored in Megan's hesitation. It was a mistake he would never have made in a business deal, but dammit, the woman had gotten under his skin. He was trying too goddamn hard, and he knew it. But somehow, he couldn't bring himself to back off.

He wanted her, dammit. And Parker had spent his life going after what he wanted.

He didn't intend to stop now.

"Megan." He'd released her hand after they'd gotten out of the car, and now he reached for her again. She avoided him though, crossing her arms over her chest as if blocking a chill. A ridiculous notion in the middle of an Austin summer.

"Tell me what you're thinking."

There was a pause, but then she answered, her eyes still on the jet. "I'm thinking that I wasn't expecting a plane. A car, sure. A taxi, maybe. Even a horse drawn carriage around downtown. But Parker, a plane?" She turned to face him. "I'm not sure that I should—"

"Do you trust me?"

"What? I—It's not about that."

"Of course it is. You're standing here trying to decide if it's wise to get on a plane with a man who's trying very hard to seduce you."

Her throat moved as she swallowed. "Maybe."

Well, that was progress. He pulled out his phone. "I don't own this jet," he said. "I'm just renting it. This is the contract," he added, showing her the screen. He opened a text message and forwarded it to her. "Send it to Griffin. Send it to all your friends. Send it to Kasey back in Los Angeles."

Her eyes widened at that. "You remember Kasey?"

"The friend from your apartment building. She came to a few parties with you."

"Well, that certainly explains a lot."

He shook his head, not understanding.

"How you managed to become such a big deal businessman so fast. You have a seriously impressive memory."

It was true, he thought. He did. But it was the most impressive when it was focused on facts and people that he cared about.

"The point is that the contract has all the information about the plane and the pilot. You're nervous about flying off and disappearing from Austin, but you don't have to be." This time, he did take her hand, and she let him. "You can trust me," he said. "I promise."

"I do trust you."

Those simple words filled him with more joy than he'd expected.

"I'm just not sure I trust myself."

He saw the shadow in her eye and was sure she

was thinking of Carlton. "But you do trust your-self," he pointed out. "That's why you're in Austin. That's why you came to talk to me about the contest. That's why you're not dating Griffin even though it would be so easy to fall into that pattern with a friend."

"I think you're seeing serendipity more than me trusting my instincts. But it's a sweet thought," she added, before he could argue.

She lifted her head to focus on the plane, then drew in a deep breath even as he held his in antic-ipation.

"Will you tell me where we're going?"

"If you want me to."

"No," she said, squeezing his hand. "You're right. I do trust myself. And I trust you, too." She met his eyes, then smiled. "Wait to tell me until we're in the air."

THE SURPRISE, it turned out, was New Orleans, someplace Megan had never been, and so she was completely giddy when he told her that it was only an hour flight, and that they'd be having a late dinner at Commander's Palace before returning to the French Quarter for a night of jazz, drinks, and dancing.

Giddy, yes. But also confused.

Because despite the electricity that zinged between them—despite the fact that they'd been sitting side by side on the plush leather loveseat for a good fifteen minutes now—Parker hadn't made any sort of move to seduce her. Hell, he hadn't even touched her, and, frankly, she missed the way his finger had felt when he'd teased her thigh in the car.

And her body still ached from the way he'd eased her skirt up, his fingers coming so deliciously close to her sex that it had taken all of her willpower not to either squirm or beg.

Not to mention those sensual, seductive words with which he'd teased her. Words that had melted her, making her long for more than just talk.

But now, as they soared over Texas and Louisiana, he made no move at all. And, dammit, his lack of attention was starting to give her a complex. Especially after she'd logged onto the plane's wifi in order to text Griffin to find out who won the contest—Parker, of course—and he'd flat out told her to use a condom, to get at least a little sleep, and for God's sake not to lay her heart on the line.

Ironic that neither her heart nor her sleep schedule were at risk, and at the moment a condom would only be useful for making balloon animals.

She'd ended the text conversation by asking him to feed the cats and the fish. And then, since Parker's mention of Kasey had brought her to the forefront of her mind, she'd texted her LA bestie, telling her that Megan was currently heading to New Orleans with Parker Manning, and would wonders never cease?

Kasey, of course, would assume that sex was on the menu. And the fact that it wasn't even an appetizer was what finally spurred Megan to her feet and to action.

That, and the fact that she'd just finished her second glass of wine and boldness came easier with alcohol.

"This," she said, as she stood in front of him, "isn't at all what I expected."

"No?"

His expression was innocent, but she thought she saw heat underneath his stoic facade. Heat, and possibly amusement. As if they were in the center of a cosmic joke and she was the one who didn't get the punch line. A possibility that, frankly, only added to her frustration.

"No," she said firmly. "From the moment I stepped into your office, sensual words fell from your lips like honey. I mean, honestly, you could qualify for the dirty talk Hall of Fame. But that's all I get? Talk? Haven't you heard what they say about all talk and no action?"

The corner of his mouth curved up, and heat bloomed in his eyes. "You're saying you thought I'd touch you? That I'd slowly strip you, then tease every inch of you mercilessly with my tongue? That I'd kiss you until you were breathless and wet and ready. That I'd stretch you open with my fingers, then thrust my cock inside you and ride you wild and hard until you begged for mercy? Is that what you thought, Megan?"

Her breath came faster with each word, and her legs went weak. "That's what I'm talking about," she finally said, despite the fact that her mouth had gone dry. Her sex, she noticed, wasn't dry at all. Not anymore. "All talk, no action. Well, enough of that."

She saw his eyes go wide and heard his sharp intake of breath as she moved to him then straddled his lap. Her skirt spread in the process, and the hard length of his erection pressed firm against her sex, separated only by his jeans and her panties.

His arousal spurred her on. *This* was what he wanted; she was certain of it. Her coming to him. Surrendering, just as he'd said in his office. Now here she was, open and ready, willing to give herself to him. Wanting the decadent sensation of his wickedly dirty words coming to life.

Victory coiled through her. He'd used that verbal seduction to make her wet and wanting. But the game was that it was all on her. He'd promised her pleasure she couldn't imagine and assured her that she'd beg for his mercy. But he'd also made no secret that he wanted her submission, and she was giving it to him.

She eased her hips back and forth, stroking herself against him, certain she was winning when she saw his eyes turn hard with the kind of need that required fast action and hard kisses.

"Megan. Oh, Christ, Megan."

"Yes," she murmured, grinding against him. She rocked her hips so that his erection stroked her sex and teased her clit, making all the thoughts in her head evaporate, leaving only a wild, violent need. She was shameless. Wet. Desperate.

More than that, she was determined, and she reached for his fly.

He wanted her surrender—well, dammit, he had it. He'd promised her a pleasure so intense it would make her scream, and she wanted that, too. She'd come this far with him—it was time for Parker to take her the rest of the way.

In case he'd missed the point, she started to tug down his zipper, but his hands caught hers, stilling them, his touch gentle, but firm.

Finally. She allowed herself a little smile, certain that this was it. Now he was going to take what he wanted.

But all he said was, "Later." And that simple word shattered her soul.

She stared at him, speechless.

"Not now," he whispered. "Not like this."

"Not like this?" she snapped, embarrassment welling up inside her. "Not like what? You seduce me onto a plane and then turn me down? What kind of screwed up game are you playing?" She scrambled off him, terrified that she'd made a horrible mistake. That Parker was more messed up than Carlton, and that she was trapped in the air, completely at his mercy.

Which was where you wanted to be just minutes ago, remember?

She stumbled across the aisle to a single seat, then closed her eyes, pulled her knees up and hugged them to her chest. Mortification coursed through her, and her cheeks burned with embarrassment. She'd opened herself. She'd let herself *want*. And he'd completely shut her down.

"You bastard," she whispered, her eyes burning as she opened them to look at him. But she was determined not to cry.

"Megan, I'm sorry. You don't understand. Right now, I don't think there's anything I want more than to rip off those damn panties and have you ride me all the way to New Orleans. But we can't. Not yet. I let us both get out of control, but—"

"Shut up," she whispered as the plane started to descend and tears leaked from her eyes. "Just shut up and take me home."

Chapter Seven

PARKER KEPT a tight rein on control even though he wanted to lash out—not at her, but at himself. He'd made a goddamn mess of things, and in the process he'd hurt her. A horrible, ironic outcome considering he'd planned this trip with the specific goal telling her how much he craved her.

"I can't take you home now," he said, working to keep his frustration out of his voice. "It's too late for the jet to take off. But if you still want to leave in the morning, we can be gone as early as eight."

"Good," she said. "Plan on it."

The plane was in the hanger now, and she moved to the open exit door without waiting for him, then started down the stairs. By the time he caught up with her at the hired car, the driver had already opened the back door, and she'd slid into the slick black Lincoln.

When he joined her, she started to slide the rest of the way across the bench seat to open the opposite door and get out. "I think I'll sit up front."

"No," he said, pressing his hand to her thigh to still her. She looked at his hand, then at his face, her eyes cold. "Stay," he ordered, in a voice that allowed no argument.

He saw her swallow, then watched as she fastened her seatbelt, then leaned back, her arms crossed over her chest as if in protection. *From him.*

Slowly, he took three deep breaths, trying to temper his emotions and calm his mind.

"I assume we're going straight to the hotel? I'm really not in the mood for dinner or jazz."

"The Ritz-Carlton," he told the driver, who lifted a hand to his cap in a silent salute, then pulled out of the hanger and headed toward the heart of the city.

They drove in silence, and it was only when there were miles of distance between them and the airport that he said, "I was nineteen when I walked away from my father's money."

She continued to stare straight ahead, but her posture shifted almost imperceptibly, and Parker hoped that meant she was listening. "My sister-in-law had filed for a restraining order against my brother. It turns out he was beating the shit out of her."

Now, she turned toward him, then drew a breath as her eyes dipped down to the hands she had clasped in her lap. "My sister was married to a man like your brother. And watching her suffer and make excuses was like…" She trailed off with a shake of her head, then lifted her head to look at him. "I swore I'd never let that happen to me. It escalates. It always escalates. First sign he's trouble, and that's the end as far as I'm concerned."

He nodded, wondering if she put him in the *trouble* category. And hoping that she didn't. "A good policy. But not your sister's, I'm guessing."

She shook her head. "No. She got out, but she stayed too long. She—she's not the same woman she used to be. She has sharp edges now. And a lot of scars—the kind you can't see, but they're there."

He knew the kind of scars she meant.

"What happened with your sister-in-law?" she asked. "Did she get out?"

"She filed for divorce and she pressed charges. Assault. Battery. Rape. My family's powerful, and the money—well, my father could have funded a thousand defenses and not even made a dent in our financial wherewithal. My father might be a prick, but he's a brilliant one."

"Defenses," she repeated. "You're saying that your father financed your brother's defense. Even though he attacked and raped his wife? Or was she making stuff up to try for a settlement?"

"I saw her in the hospital." He closed his eyes to block the horrific memory. "She wasn't faking."

"Your father couldn't see that? Couldn't believe that his son would do that?"

"Oh, he believed it. He just couldn't let something that sordid soil the family name. After all, the little tramp was messing with our family. That meant we had to destroy her."

She licked her lips. "We?"

"Or so my father insisted. The family had to stick together. My mother, my sister, me. Even though my brother had always been a violent son-of-a-bitch, because he had the Manning last name, the wagons had to circle."

"What happened?"

"My brother got off without even a slap on the wrist. My sister-in-law got her divorce and not a single dime. I'm pretty sure she was fine with that, so long as she was free. My mother sank further into her shell, and my older sister and I cut ties with the family. Permanently."

"But—" She cut herself off, and he could practically see the questions churning in her mind. "But everyone says you used your family money to get your start. That's how PCM Enterprises was funded."

"*No*." The word came out sharper than he intended, but he'd worked his ass off to make that dream a reality, and while he could deal with the general public having the wrong idea, he needed Megan to understand the truth.

"I inherited some money from my grandfather. Most people would say it's a lot, but in my family it's a pittance. But it's all I took with me. That money, my clothes, and a few books."

"Is that when you moved to LA?"

She was listening intently now, and he tried not to show how much he hoped they were over the roadblock that his idiocy had thrown in their path.

"I ended up at UCLA, and while I was there I invested pretty well." That was an understatement. He'd quadrupled his money when he sold his interest in a biotech company, then did essentially the same thing a few years later, once he was out of college.

After that, he'd invested a portion of his money conservatively, but used the bulk of it to get PCM Enterprises off the ground. Initially, it was based in Los Angeles, but as he grew more and more disillusioned with the crowd he hung with, he made the decision to move back to Texas. Not to Houston where his parents still lived, but to Austin, where he'd gone to high school at a private boarding school.

"The rest," he concluded after telling her as much, "is history."

They rode in silence for a while, thoughts churning in Parker's head. Memories of a time not too long ago when he'd still been living in LA. When he'd distanced himself from men like Carlton, and yet their paths had still intersected, not in small part because Carlton was the kind of man who was drawn to money and power. He had just enough of both to be dangerous, and not enough to truly understand either.

And at the time, Parker was still enjoying all the perks that his bankroll offered him, not yet realizing that when he breathed in that life, the reason he felt so damn suffocated was because he was living in a vacuum. And nothing survives like that.

Looking back, Parker despised the man he'd

been in Los Angeles, at least in those early years. Megan had known him then, or at least tangentially, and it bothered him that she surely remembered the Parker from the past—the one who would have just plowed forward without thinking about what Megan might want, the one who went through women and money like candy—and only now was getting to know the Parker he'd worked so hard to become.

He wanted to say something, to explain how much he'd changed. But they'd arrived and the Town Car was pulling to a stop. Before the valet could open the door, he took her hand, relieved when she didn't pull it away.

He hadn't yet explained why he'd pulled away on the plane. But maybe—just maybe—he'd managed to crawl part of the way out of the doghouse.

Chapter Eight

SINCE THEY HAD NO BAGS, it was easy to slide straight from the car and into the lobby. No one paid them any attention, of course, but Megan still felt as if all eyes were on them. After all, they'd arrived at a hotel with no luggage. Which could only mean one thing.

Or, at least, when they'd left Austin she'd assumed it would only mean one thing. Now she wasn't sure. He'd revealed a part of himself in the car, and she knew that somehow he was leading up to an explanation of what happened. Of why he'd pushed her away when they'd both so clearly wanted each other.

But that didn't change the fact that her ego was still bruised.

While she stood near the massive flower

arrangement that dominated the lobby, Parker went to the front desk to check-in. It only took a minute —he'd gone to a VIP desk that apparently had the perk of supersonic speed—and was back at her side before her ping-ponging nerves had settled.

"I don't know about you," he said, "but I'd like a drink." He nodded to the lobby bar. "Shall we?"

He started that direction, but she pulled him back by the hem of *The Fix on Sixth* T-shirt that he still wore. "Forget it, Cowboy. I need some answers. First you practically seduce me at the same time that you scold me in your office, and you punctuate that encounter by telling me that you want me. And then when I'm down with that program and about to earn my membership in the Mile High Club, you shut me down fast. And while I get that there's a reason buried in the life story you were sharing with me, I haven't really heard it yet."

She'd started her spiel in a low whisper, but emotion had made her voice rise, and she realized they were attracting a few interested looks.

She stepped closer and lowered her voice again. "Forget the long explanation, okay? I know it's cheating, but I want to skip straight to the end of the mystery. So just tell me the bottom line, already. Because dammit Parker, I was throwing myself at you, and my ego is now in desperate need of an icepack and some Tylenol."

He smiled at that, which was her intent, because the conversation had gotten a little too real in the car. She truly did want to understand him—heck, the more time she spent with him, the more she wanted to know how he ticked, this man who'd walked away from one fortune only to build another on his own terms.

But right now, it wasn't his background she was concerned with. It was his libido. Because despite the fact that he'd pushed the abort button, now that her fury had settled, her own libido was back in gear and ready for launch. "Truth time, Parker. Did you mean what you said? Do you want me or not?"

He took a single step back, then lifted his hand to her hair, running the long strands through his fingers. "Do I want you?" His voice sounded tight, almost pained. "Dear God, yes. I want you desperately. I have, actually, for a very long time. But not like this."

"Like this?" she repeated, confused. "Like what?"

"Not as a demand. And definitely not as a payment."

Now she was even more confused. "But that was

the deal. That's what we agreed on, right there in your office. Just a little inappropriate office conduct between consenting adults, right?"

He chuckled. "That's one way of putting it." He nodded toward the elevators. "I think we should take this upstairs."

She followed without question, her mind still whirring. "Okay, then. Tell me another," she said, when they were alone in the elevator. "Because I'm really confused right now, and have absolutely no idea what you want."

"Just like I've said all along. I want you, Megan. But I don't want a fast fuck."

He reached out to gently stroke her cheek, the contact scorching her skin and making her breath shudder.

"I've had a lot of women over the years, but not anymore. What I told you about rebuilding my reputation, I meant it. I don't fuck around anymore. And I'm damn sure not making it a game to see how many women I can get into my bed."

Her brows rose. "Did you ever?"

"A game, no. Though some of my friends did." A self-deprecating smile played at his lips. "I was more of a collector. I'd date beautiful women, and there would be an attraction. But I never got close. For the most part, I never wanted to."

He met her eyes, then held her gaze as the heat of that moment charged the air between them and awareness curled through her, all the way down to her toes. "I want to get close now, Megan."

Her head was spinning. "I—"

He cut her off with a gentle finger to her lips. "For years, I was given everything I ever wanted. When I walked away from my family's money, I learned that the only things I value are the things I've worked for. Or the people who also value me."

"Are you saying that I'm of value to you?" Behind her, the elevator doors slid open.

"Aren't you?" He took her arm, then steered her out.

"I don't know." She understood him wanting sex, but what about her caught the eye of someone like Parker? Not only wealthy, but talented and ambitious. And she was just a makeup artist scrambling to keep her head above water.

They walked in silence for a moment until they reached the room. He opened the door and they stepped into the living area of a stunning suite, with bedrooms on either side.

She stood still, not interested in the room. Only in him. "I really don't know," she repeated.

"Then let me answer the question. You are, Megan. You're of great value to me."

She tilted her head so that she could see his face better, trying to discern if this was the truth or a line. But all she saw was sincerity. And there was nothing evasive in his voice.

"Why?"

"Maybe because I think you might understand what I've accomplished. What I'm still trying to accomplish."

She shook her head. "I don't know what you mean."

"Well, look what you've done. You left a job at Sephora at an Oklahoma City mall at twenty-one and went to LA by yourself with nothing but a dream and a little bit of cash."

"How did you—"

"You worked three jobs while you got your cosmetology license, then you ordered a box of business cards and offered a card to pretty much everyone you met. The business grew slowly, but it grew, and by the time you turned twenty-six, you had a solid career working with portrait photographers before shoots and name brand celebrities before events."

She hugged herself, each of his revelations hanging heavy between them as she thought of Carlton and his fixation on her. "How do you know all that?"

His smile seemed entirely innocent. "I collect information, Megan. As far as business goes, it's my secret weapon."

"Business," she repeated. "You mean the contest?"

"I wanted to get a sense of you. And I happen to know a few of your clients. They all like to gossip. I asked, they told."

She nodded, somewhat mollified. After the flyer fiasco, she could understand him wanting to know who had screwed up and plastered his picture around town.

"I was left with a pretty good sense of your career path," Parker said. "And what you built wasn't shabby."

"Yeah, well, I don't have much of it left now." Immediately, she regretted the words. She hadn't told him why she'd run from LA, and she hadn't asked him to not tell Carlton where she was. But now he was probably going to ask why she bolted, and she really didn't want to talk about it.

But all he said was, "That's why they call it a fresh start, sweetheart. You'll build it up again. After all, you already know that you can. And gaining the confidence is the hardest part."

She peered at him, trying to discern if he knew why she'd wanted that fresh start. She couldn't tell. But at least he seemed to respect it. Which meant that he probably wasn't sending telegrams back to Los Angeles announcing where the long lost Megan Carter had got off to.

Even so, she should probably specifically mention that she was keeping a low profile and ask him not to post on social media, too. Just to be sure.

After all, loitering black cars made her twitchy. How much worse would it be if she suspected that Carlton knew where to find her? Assuming he even still cared. Which he probably didn't. It had been months; surely he'd moved on.

"It's late, Megan," he said before she'd gathered her thoughts. "And I'm tired. But here's the bottom line. I'm not interested in a fast fuck. I don't do that anymore. But I'm also not proposing marriage. Hell, I'm not even asking you to go steady. All I'm saying is that I want you for more than one night.

You fascinate me, Megan. You always have. You light a fire inside me, and unless I'm mistaken, I think I make you burn, too."

He ran his fingers through his hair, looking both sexy and exhausted. "If I led you on, I'm sorry. But it was worth it to spend the time with you. And I'll get you back to Austin first thing in the morning."

He reached out and took her hand, then lifted it and pressed a soft kiss to her palm. "Your bedroom's over there. Goodnight, Megan. I'm sure I'll see you in my dreams."

Chapter Nine

NEEDLESS TO SAY, Megan couldn't sleep.

She was in *his* dreams?

Boy, could she beat that. Because Megan didn't even need to go to sleep for Parker Manning to fill her head.

Was he lying in his bed, sound asleep, while she tossed and turned, a mess of sensual longing and unfulfilled need?

Or was he, like her, lost in fantasies? Was he imagining coming to her door and slowly turning the knob? Was he closing his eyes and picturing the way she'd respond if he reached for her in the dark and gently stroked her shoulder before sitting on the edge of the bed and tugging down the sheet to reveal her bare breasts, her nipples tight and hard with desire?

She sighed, unable to ignore the insistent warm glow spreading over her body in response to her decadent thoughts. And since they'd come without luggage, she was naked under the sheet, and the cool cotton felt incredible on her overheated skin.

I want you to want me.

Was that what he'd said? Because oh, God, she did want him.

Not a fast fuck. Not a one-time thing.

Her stomach did a little flip at that. She'd been doing fine on her own in Austin. She had friends. A nice life. And she didn't have to worry about her boyfriend turning possessive and weird and creepy.

But still…

There was no denying that Parker had gotten under her skin—heck, she'd been intrigued by him even back in Los Angeles. Now they were both in Texas, and Parker Manning was even more compelling. After all, she could hardly forget Parker's heated demands and sensual descriptions of all the things he intended to do to her.

So, yeah. She wanted him.

And, yeah. He wanted her.

Which begged the question of why she was in this room and he was in the other when the whole point of coming on this trip in the first place was sex. Wild and hot and intense and *Parker*.

She sat up, the thought blinking in her head like neon.

Parker.

And that was her answer, wasn't it? Like Parker had said, it wasn't just sex that she wanted. No, she was craving the man she'd laughed with. The man whose career and history intrigued her. Whose naughty words had aroused her. Who had valued the work she'd done and understood the sacrifices she'd made.

The man who wanted *her*.

So, yeah, she was going to him.

Thankfully, the hotel had stocked her closet with a robe so she didn't have to wrap herself in a sheet like an Egyptian mummy. Instead, she snuggled into the spa-style material and then padded barefoot into the living area. The lights were off, only a single lamp on by the bar to help guide her way to his door.

And his lights were off, too, if the lack of glow from under the door was any indication.

He was probably asleep. And if he was, she probably shouldn't wake him. Because that meant he wasn't simpatico with her. Wasn't tossing and turning and thinking all sorts of wicked thoughts.

But if he *was* awake … if he was simply lying there in the dark…

Before she could talk herself out of it, she lunged for the doorknob, turned it, and pushed open the door.

"Megan."

Every muscle in her body relaxed at the sound of his voice, thick with a desire so familiar it seemed to burn through her.

"Did you mean it?" she whispered, standing still in the doorway. "Or was it just a line? To make you seem all honorable and awesome?"

"Not a line," he said, propping himself up in bed, his face and chest illuminated by the thin glow of light that crept in from the living area. "But if you're asking if I want you, then God yes. I'm hard as steel from thinking about you in the other room, and I swear I was about to lose my mind knowing there wasn't a damn thing I could do about it."

She leaned against the door, amused. "I'm pretty sure there was *something* you could have done about it."

"Maybe," he agreed. "But why fly solo when I can have a copilot?" He stood up, the sheet falling away. She drew in a breath, mesmerized by the way the light and shadows played on his rock-hard erection and the tight, hard muscles of his body.

"Please," she said, not sure what she was asking for, just knowing she wanted it all. *Needed* it all.

His eyes swept slowly over her, his inspection so intense it seemed to burn through her robe, leaving her skin prickly in its wake. "Take it off," he said.

The words were a command, and she wouldn't dream of disobeying. She let the robe fall back, and she heard his groan of appreciation as he stepped toward her.

"Christ, you're beautiful." He moved to within inches of her, his scent enveloping her, making her even wetter. Her body was on fire, every cell primed for his touch. And when he reached out and traced his fingertip over the swell of her breast, she arched back and cried aloud.

"So damn responsive. Baby, you're amazing."

"Parker."

"Tell me what you want." His soft voice caressed her, as intimate as his touch. "Why did you come here, naked in the night?"

"I want you," she said, because she had to be honest, and that was as real as it got. "You promised me so much, but the only thing I really want is to feel you inside me."

His mouth curved up as his finger eased down along the swell of her breast before continuing down, making her bite her lower lip when he gently traced her navel. Then lower and lower, until he brushed her clit, and she gasped, then sucked in air as his finger thrust deep into her core. "Is that how you want me inside you?"

Her hips moved of their own volition, and she ground against him. "Yes. No. I want everything."

"Oh, baby," he said. "So do I." For a second, he met her eyes, and she almost stumbled, knocked over by the intensity of the passion she saw there. "Right now, I need to taste you."

A shiver curled through her as he moved closer, then slid his fingers into her hair to hold her steady. He kissed her, his mouth claiming hers. The kind of kiss that stole reason and fired passion and made her entire body ache.

She didn't want it to stop, but when he pulled away, he continued to do such amazing things with his lips and tongue that she couldn't quite manage a protest. He suckled her neck, making her crazed, then drew his mouth lower, his lips grazing the fine line of her collarbone before moving down to her breast.

The tip of his tongue teased her nipple, but it was when he closed his mouth over her and sucked hard that she almost lost it. Her hands were on his shoulders so she could hold herself steady, and in that moment, she squeezed so hard she was certain she'd leave finger-sized bruises.

He pulled back, her nipple popping free from his lips, and the sensation of cool air on her damp skin made her tremble with fresh need. "You like that," he said, and since it wasn't a question, she didn't answer. Words were too much work at that point.

"Let's see how you like this." Slowly, he eased to his knees, then used one hand to hold her steady while the other gently urged her legs apart. She moaned, but complied, then gasped as his head dipped, and his tongue teased and explored her pussy, laving and stroking and working her clit.

She twined her fingers in his hair, using the contact to anchor herself, because God knew her legs had gone week. She kept her eyes closed until she was certain she could control the waves of pleasure crashing through her. But when he added to the sensual onslaught by thrusting a finger deep inside her, finding her most sensitive spots, she moaned, and made noises she didn't even know she could make. And when his tongue hit exactly *that* spot, the only reason she didn't either fall to the floor or fly up to the heavens was that he was there to hold her tight.

For what felt like an eternity, pleasure accosted her, making her dizzy. And, yes, making her crave even more of him.

"My turn," she said when the world had righted and she could manufacture a coherent thought again. And before he had a chance to ask what she meant, she fell to her knees.

"Oh, no, Angel," he said, pulling her up. "I like the idea, but let's take this to the bed." He led her there, and she straddled him, then took him into her mouth, his cock growing even harder as she licked and sucked, the low groans of pleasure he was making as arousing to her as his touch had been.

She didn't want to stop—he was so close, but he tangled his hand into her hair, and pulled her up to him. Their eyes met, and for a moment she thought she saw the future reflected in his gorgeous eyes. She was being ridiculous, of course, but the thought didn't scare her. Nothing about Parker scared her.

"Is this real?" she whispered, but it was only when the words had passed her lips that she realized she'd spoken aloud.

"As real as it gets." He brushed a kiss over her lips.

"And tomorrow? When we get back to Austin?"

"Are you asking me if this is a one-off? If I like to fly my one-night stands to New Orleans and show them a good time at my favorite hotel?"

Her cheeks burned. "Please don't tease me. Not like this."

"Oh, baby." He stroked her cheek. "No, I shouldn't tease you. And no, this isn't a one-off. Not if I have anything to say about it. And no, I don't usually fly my dates out of the city."

"Really?"

His kiss was featherlight. "Really."

She licked her lips, his sweet words clinging to her, adding a new dimension to the heat that flowed in her veins. "Those things you said in your office," she began. "Will you—I mean, will you take me higher?"

Her cheeks burned, but she didn't regret the words. She wanted everything he'd teased her with. The full on-slaught of pleasure.

He tilted his head, then inspected her naked body.

And as she watched, his expression changed. Still aroused, still lit with the fire of passion. But there was something else, too. Something possessive. Controlling. And for the first time she understood what he meant when he'd said he wanted her submission.

"All right," he finally said, and the intensity in his voice sent a shiver rushing through her. "On your hands and knees. On the bed. Facing the headboard."

Anticipation cut through her, making her core clench and her breasts ache. And when he stepped away, only to return with his belt, she bit her lower lip as she wondered what he intended to do with it.

"Lean forward on your elbows," he ordered. "Wrists together."

She complied, and he used the belt to encircle her wrists and then bind her to the slatted headboard.

"I thought about tying your legs, too," he told her as he got behind her on the bed. "But I think I like your ass just where it is."

She did, too, she realized when he eased up behind her, his hard cock sliding between her thighs so that the shaft rubbed her intimately.

"Baby, you are so wet," he said, and as he spoke,

he rocked his hips, so that his erection just barely teased her clit and his fingers stroked her perineum, teasing her a little by rimming the tight muscle at her ass.

She gasped when he slipped his finger tip inside her, and he made a soft sound of approval. "I think we'll have to save that for later. I don't want you to come too quickly."

He was right; the unusual sensation had pushed her that much closer to the edge, and now she was fully aware, every cell in her body primed to go over the edge. And when he bent over her, his chest to her back and his hands on her nipples, she thought that the only thing she wanted was to be bound to him forever.

His lips teased the back of her neck, a spot more erotic than she'd ever imagined, and his fingers pinched her nipples, the pressure tight—almost too intense—and though she tried to twist away, with her hands bound, there was only so far she could go. Only so far she wanted to go, really, because with each pinch and tease, she felt the hot wire of pleasure zing down to her core.

She was throbbing now, and she was certain she was dripping with need. Her pussy clenched in a sensual rhythm, wanting him inside her. Wanting to be filled.

He pinched her nipple tighter, and she cried out, a deep, pleasure-filled cry of, "Yes!"

"I like the way you respond," he said. "Have you ever been spanked?"

She shook her head. Carlton wanted to, but she'd refused. Even then, before the weirdness, she couldn't go there with him. But with Parker...

She bit her lower lip. She hadn't expected it, but just the thought made her sex tingle and ache. "Please," she said before he even asked. And his answer was nothing more than a low groan of satisfaction.

He shifted, releasing her breasts as he slipped one hand under her lower belly, holding her in place. "It's more intense because you're bound," he said. "But I want to take you there. To that line between pain and pleasure. I want the sting of my palm to linger on your ass as you balance on that knife-edge. And when I fuck you, I want you to tumble over into pleasure, all the more intense because you've touched its counterpart."

She wanted to answer, but her throat was too thick with anticipation, and when he got behind her and rubbed her ass, she sucked in a breath. And when his palm came down with a smack on her skin, sending prickles of awareness through her, she arched up and moaned as the heat of his hand seemed to cut through to her aching, needy sex.

"Oh, baby, you're so fucking beautiful. More?"

"Yes." Her voice was tight. "Please."

He complied, taking her higher each time his palm connected with her tender flesh until she was dripping with desire and tugging at her bindings, wanting to free her hands so she could stroke her clit, touch herself, make herself come.

"Now," he said, and then one hand was on her hip and with his other, he was guiding his cock into her core. She tried to shift her position, making them fit better, but he had complete control of her, and she gasped, crying out his name as he thrust inside her in a timeless rhythm as his hand reached between them and he teased her clit.

He was right, the intensity of their connection was so much more when her skin was so hyper-aware, but even so, she wanted to see him. To face him.

As if reading her mind, he said, "I'm untying you. I want to watch her face. I can't take you from behind the first time, Megan. I need your face. I have to watch you go over."

"Yes," she said, as he hurried to unfasten her, and she flipped over onto her back noticing that at some point he'd sheathed himself with a condom.

"On me," he said, moving beside her and urging her to straddle him. "And hurry, baby. I have to be inside you, Megan. I'm about to lose it." And since she wanted it as much as he did, she hurried on top of him, easing down, and then rising up again, over and over, riding him with the help of his hands on her hips.

He was so deep, and it felt so good, and she saw his coming orgasm in the fierce expression on that beautiful face. "Please," she begged. "I want to feel you explode."

He came then, his bucking body taking her close to the edge once more. And though she didn't think she'd go over again, when he teased her clit with one hand and teased the rim of her ass with the other, she completely shattered, abandoning reason to passion and losing herself to the onslaught of pleasure.

They clung to each other for hours after that, just breathing and dozing and enjoying the feel of skin on skin.

He roused her with kisses before dawn and took her to Café du Monde for coffee and beignets before they walked along the Mississippi as the sun rose.

They spent the day talking and laughing, their conversation covering everything and nothing. He told her about the challenges of running a company, and she told him about how she dreamed of one day having her own skincare and makeup line. "It's a big step to go from doing someone's makeup to creating my own line, though."

"If you want it badly enough, you'll figure it out. And fortunately you happen to know a brilliant businessman who can answer all your questions."

"Do I?"

"Well, he'll answer them for a price. One kiss per question."

She raised her brows, letting her gaze drop to his crotch then back to his face. "A bargain. I would have willingly paid so much more."

"Well, you can always offer him a tip," he said, before pulling her to him and exacting the negotiated payment in advance.

He took her on the trolley to Camellia Grille in the Garden District where they ate burgers before strolling down the lovely streets and checking out the homes. They wandered for hours, their conversation never stalling, until they finally caught the trolley back to the French Quarter.

There, they wandered the market, trying on masks and silly sunglasses, then took a horse-drawn carriage around the Quarter.

It was a lovely day. Perfect, really. And though she didn't want it to end, at seven, they headed back to the jet, and she paused on the stairs. "Thank you," she said. "This was the best punishment ever."

He laughed, and once they were inside the plane and belted in, she leaned against him. His arm went around her and she closed her eyes.

She was asleep even before the jet left the ground, feeling warm and content and absolutely wonderful.

Chapter Ten

"HOW'S IT GOING, LADIES?" Tyree asked as he stepped into his office. Megan and Eva Anderson had commandeered his desk to look at various images from around Austin as they brainstormed where in town they wanted to photograph the various men of the month for the calendar.

"Not bad," Eva said, leaning back against him as he slid his arms around her. A big bear of a man, his hug engulfed Eva, but it was clear she didn't mind. The photographer recently moved from Seattle to Austin after reconnecting with Tyree, the father of her grown daughter, Elena.

Secure in his arms, she tilted her head back and smiled broadly at him. "Take a peek," she said, indicating the printed images scattered over the desktop and the virtual images on the computer screen.

"We'll go to the actual locations with all you winners, of course," Megan said. "And we're shooting the first six winners tomorrow. Right now, we're planning to shoot from the Loop 360 bridge with the river in the background, the Capitol grounds, Mount Bonnell, the stone cows at the Arboretum, Lake Travis, and someplace on campus. We're not sure where, though."

"All sounds good. And why don't you shoot from the South Mall? Put a guy on the steps and get the Tower in the background."

The women exchanged glances and nodded. "Perfect," Eva said.

"Which man's getting which location? Personally, I want the Capitol."

"All for all," Megan said. "That way we have more choices for the calendar."

Tyree chuckled. "Fair enough. And we're doing this all tomorrow? It's going to be a crazy day."

Megan didn't disagree, but she did tell him that Taylor had managed to borrow a van. "So at least we'll all be together and no one will get lost in traffic."

"We're doing each of the men inside The Fix,

too," Eva told him. "And outside on the street with the facade behind them."

"I think you two have this well in hand." He smiled, his attention on Eva, who rose up on her toes and kissed him.

"Off you go, man," she said. "You're distracting me. But I'll see you at home. You're working late?"

"Not tonight. Reece is closing. I'll be home by eight. And," he added, "Eli's staying over at a friend's."

Eva shot Megan a grin before turning back to her fiancé. "That, Mr. Johnson, is some very interesting information."

He chuckled, then said goodbye to both of them, pausing beside Megan before heading out. He pressed a paternal hand to her shoulder. "I'm sorry about what happened with Parker. But looks like it all turned out okay, yeah?"

"Hmm? Oh. Yeah." She nodded. "Things are totally squared away."

"Glad to hear it," Tyree said, then headed out of the office with one final kiss toward Eva.

She returned it, then cocked her head. "Squared away? Girl, I think that might be an understatement."

Megan stood up straighter. "I haven't the

slightest idea what you're talking about," she said, but she couldn't maintain it. And within a minute, both she and Eva were laughing and comparing notes about the men in their lives.

Barely twenty-four hours had passed since she and Parker had returned from New Orleans, and they'd spent most of those hours together in his downtown condo. They'd split a bottle of wine and watched a movie in his bed yesterday afternoon, pausing it from time to time when their chatter about the movie blossomed into a longer conversation.

Of course, that made the movie go longer than three hours, so it was late by the time it was over, and it seemed prudent to skip dinner and stay in bed. They'd made love slowly, almost lazily. After, Megan had fallen asleep on her side with Parker spooned around her and had awakened to the smell of coffee brewing and bacon frying.

That was nice enough, but when she stumbled into the kitchen and saw him flipping bacon in briefs and a Kiss the Cook apron, her heart had flipped over. And in that moment, whatever this thing was between her and Parker ratcheted up another notch, leaving her feeling warm and safe and happy.

So maybe Eva was right. Not that Megan was going to say so out loud, though. Instead, she kept the sweet secret bottled inside, and went through the day with a smile on her face.

An hour later, Megan was walking home, and since she was still thinking about the way she'd described Parker to Eva—funny, charming, and so sexy it should be a crime—she decided to go the long way home so that she could pop in and surprise Parker at his condo, which was on the opposite side of downtown from hers. He'd told her he was going to spend the day working from home, then would head over to her place for dinner.

Unless he'd left early to run an errand, she should be able to catch him, and then they could walk over to The Railyard together.

She was just turning south onto Congress Avenue when her cell phone rang. She snatched it out of her purse, assuming it would be Parker, then squealed with delight when she saw that it was Kasey.

"Finally! I text you to tell you I'm actually going out with Parker Manning, and it takes you this long to get back to me?"

"You wouldn't believe how busy I've been. I

swear, I've stressed off at least five pounds. This new job is the best weight loss program ever."

Megan rolled her eyes but didn't ask. By the next time they talked, Kasey would have moved on to another best job ever.

"I can't believe you actually went out with Parker. How was it? Did you sleep with him? Is he amazing?"

Megan tried to get a word in, but luck wasn't with her. It rarely was where Kasey's chatter was concerned.

"But do me a fave, okay? Be. Careful."

"Careful?" Megan blurted the word, determined to squeeze the question in. "What are you talking about?"

"After you left, there were all these rumors about him."

She frowned. "What kind of rumors?"

"Nasty stuff. That he'd stalked this guy—or maybe it was a girl. I'm not sure. And that he was actually arrested. For assault!"

"No way."

Her body felt cold, her skin as prickly as if she'd jumped into a frozen pond. "That's ridiculous. Parker Manning? It would have made the papers.

You would have seen something official. And I would have heard about it on social media."

"Dunno. Maybe. I mean, remember what town we're talking about. This is LA. Coverup city, right?"

"I don't believe it," she said stubbornly. But even as she spoke the words, she remembered what Parker himself had said about all the shit his brother pulled—and how all it had taken was Daddy's checkbook to keep it out of the papers and the courts.

"No," she said again, but this time more weakly.

"You're probably right. I mean, you know the rumor mill out here. Oh! That reminds me. I have not told anyone where you are. You know that, right? I mean, you trust me?"

"Of course. Why?"

"It's just that I can't believe Carlton would go there. I mean, it's been months. Why would he?"

"Yeah," Megan said, her voice full of trepidation. "Why would he? And why would you even think it's a possibility?"

"Only because there's this picture floating around now. You and Parker."

"What?" How had she missed that? "From

where?" She closed her eyes, hoping it wasn't from New Orleans. That it wasn't an intimate kiss on the banks of the Mississippi.

"That bar in Austin that you're working at. He's shirtless—and holy freak, does he look good. And you're standing right beside him."

"Oh." She exhaled, trying to process the implications.

"The name of the bar is clear, so if Carlton wanted to find it, he wouldn't have any trouble at all."

"No," Megan said, frowning. "It wouldn't." She shook off the funk. "But you know what? You're right. Why would he? By now, I'm old news to Carlton."

"That's what I figure."

"Listen, I need to go." She'd reached the corner and had been loitering so they could finish the call. "Talk to you again soon?"

"Hell, yeah. I miss you."

"Me, too," she assured her friend, then hung up. She drew in a breath and tried to gather her thoughts, reassuring herself that Carlton wasn't coming and that Parker hadn't beat anyone up. Or if he had, then it was for a damn good reason.

She turned right on Third Street and continued on a few blocks, thinking that she'd just ask him about it. Surely he'd tell her.

His building was one of the modern high rise condos that had sprung up like chrome and glass weeds all over downtown throughout the past decade. Now, she stood across Third Street from the glass entrance, waiting for the one-way traffic to clear so she could jaywalk over to his building and see if he was home.

A moment later, though, she saw him emerge onto the sidewalk with a lovely redhead at his side. Even from across the street, Megan could see the intense affection in her eyes. That was enough to have her mouth going dry. But then her stomach dropped all the way to her knees when he pulled her into an embrace and kissed her.

Granted, the woman had turned before the kiss so that her back was to Megan, but even though she couldn't tell if it was a full-on mouth kiss complete with tongue, she could definitely tell that the hug was exuberant.

Whoever she was, she was no stranger to Parker. Not only that, but he seemed to adore her.

All of which made her stomach twist. Especially

since this revelation of a cuddly bitch in his life was laid out next to Kasey's news about assault.

Could it be true, after all? And who was the woman?

And had she been an idiot for trusting her feelings and falling hard for Parker Fucking Manning?

Chapter Eleven

BY THE TIME she got back to Congress Avenue, Megan had convinced herself that there was nothing going on between Parker and the woman.

By the time she'd reached the pedestrian gate to The Railyard, she was convinced that they were in a long-term affair, and Megan was nothing more than his piece on the side.

By the time she was in her kitchen, and the sauce was simmering, and the water for spaghetti was sitting on low heat, she didn't know what to think. All she knew was that she was a mess, and that for the last forty-five minutes, she'd been alternating between crying and scolding herself for jumping to conclusions. Even the cat had looked at her like she was crazy. The fish, thank goodness, seemed to have no opinion at all

When seven o'clock rolled around, and he hadn't arrived, she told herself that he'd dumped her, forgotten to tell her, and had run off with the redhead.

Stop it. Just stop it.

Frustrated with herself, she picked up the phone and dialed Griffin, who answered on the first ring.

"You owe me a drink," he said.

She tried to laugh, but it came out choked.

Immediately, his tone shifted to concern. "Are you okay?"

"I—yes. Sure." She scrunched her eyes closed, grimacing. She shouldn't have called Griff. He was already overly protective of her. And what if turned out to be nothing?

No. Correction. It *would* turn out to be nothing. And if she went and dumped all of her Parker problems on Griffin, then how were the two of them supposed to end up being friends?

"Christ, Megan. I can practically hear the wheels turning. What's going on? Or, rather, what's going on that you don't want to tell me?"

Why, why, why hadn't she called Taylor or Mina instead?

"It's nothing. Really. Just me being insecure."

Griff exhaled loudly. "Am I going to have to come punch Manning in the face? Because I have to be honest, I'd rather not. I mean, I've been working out, but I think he could take me."

She couldn't help it; she burst out laughing. "It's probably me being stupid. I saw him with someone earlier, and it looked like—well, I think he was kissing her."

"And what did he say when you asked him what was going on?"

"Yeah, about that…"

He sighed. "Okay, listen. All I know about the guy is he swooped you off to New Orleans for what I can only assume were kinky shenanigans."

"They so were not!" A lie, yes, but a prudent one.

"But you came back in one piece and, honestly, you looked pretty pleased with yourself. And you've only had good things to say about the guy."

"Because he's a good guy."

"So there you go. Despite my very real threat to bash his face in if he so much as hurts your feelings, I was about to say that he seems like a good guy to me. And you've been telling me he's a good guy. So why are you suddenly robbing the poor man of the benefit of the doubt and wrapping him up in your weird girly shit?"

"Excuse me?"

"Honestly, Kelsey does the same thing," he said, referring to his sister.

"This is not weird girly shit. He was kissing her."

"You think. And you haven't asked him why."

All true. "You know what? Forget it. I'm sorry I even called you."

He laughed. "No, you're not. You love me. Because even when I'm right, I don't say I told you so. And I promise not to say it tomorrow when you tell me I was right."

She rolled her eyes. "Hanging up now."

"Love you, too." And then the line went dead.

"Asshole," she muttered, but she felt a million times better. So much so that when Parker finally did arrive, and she buzzed him through the gate, she was actually smiling.

"Hey, beautiful," he said, swooping an arm around her and pulling her close so that he could kiss her very thoroughly. "That smells incredible."

"Spaghetti sauce. My mom's recipe. It's the only thing I do well in the kitchen, I warn you now."

"I think we can muddle through despite that

defect in your character." He tucked a strand of hair behind her ear, the sensation of his fingertips brushing her skin making her shiver. "How much time do we have before dinner's ready?"

"As much as we want." Already her pulse was kicking up, from nothing more than proximity to this man. "I haven't put the pasta in yet."

"Then maybe I could suggest an appetizer?" He tilted his head so that he was looking up, toward the bedroom on the second floor.

"I—" She swallowed, then took a step back out of his arms. "Oh, crap, Parker. Why were you late?"

He gaped at her, clearly befuddled. "Since when does ten minutes count as late?"

"Since now," she said. "Dammit, Parker. I must really be falling for you."

Now he looked even more confused. "Normally, I'd say that was a good thing. Why do I feel like you're about to rip me a new one?

"Usually, I hold stuff in. But with you—oh, *fuck*. Who was she, Parker? Who was the skanky bitch you were kissing earlier today?"

His brows rose, and he actually looked like he was going to laugh.

"Stop it, you jerk," she said, kicking him. Which really wasn't a good idea since she was in bare feet and the muscles of his calf were rock hard.

"Skanky, huh? Oh, this is priceless."

"Do not even pretend to not know what I'm talking about. I saw you with her. Red hair. Gorgeous. And you kissed her right in front of your condo. On the sidewalk for the whole damn world to see. Is she the reason you're late?"

"You were at my condo? Why didn't you come up?"

It was her turn to gape at him. "Um, hello? Kissing another woman? Not conducive to the whole welcoming vibe."

He slid around the breakfast bar to enter her kitchen, then poured a glass of wine from the open bottle on the counter. He passed it to her, then kept it for himself when she refused it, instead looking at him like he was insane.

He took a sip and leaned back against the counter. "The jealousy's a little cute, but you might want to cut it back just a bit."

"Dammit, Parker, you said I wasn't a one off. But the way you looked at her. Like she was someone you love. It—I mean, I—oh, hell." Her voice broke, and tears filled her eyes. She turned away, only to turn back when his hands closed on her shoulders and he gently shifted her around, then pulled her to him.

"Oh, baby," he said, holding her close and resting his chin on her head. "I'm sorry. I shouldn't have egged you on like that."

"Who was she?"

"My sister," he said gently. "And you saw me kiss her like this." He drew her close and wrapped her in a loving hug, then pressed a gentle kiss on her forehead. "Is that how you want me to kiss you?" he asked, his lips brushing her face as he asked the question, butterfly soft and so very enticing.

She shook her head, almost afraid to speak for fear of spoiling the moment.

"No? Well how about this?" Before she had a chance to respond, his mouth closed over hers, soft at first, and then hard and demanding. She parted her lips, moaning when his tongue slipped inside, tasting and teasing as the power of the kiss built and his fingers snaked through her hair, cupping the back of her head so that he could hold her still under the sensual onslaught.

It felt as though the kiss would last forever. As though it would erase all time, all space. That the world would drop away around them and there would be nothing left but her and Parker and the electricity of their connection.

She was breathing fast when he finally broke away, though his eyes stayed locked on her. She saw his chest rise and fall, and knew that his heart was pounding just as hers was.

Then he brushed her cheek and shook his head a fraction of an inch. "You have nothing—*nothing*—to be jealous of. Do you understand?"

She nodded, a little frazzled, a little giddy. "I'm sorry. I saw her and I thought—"

He held her. "I know. I know, and I'm sorry to have worried you. But baby, there's nothing to worry about." He bent his head then brushed her lips. How would you feel about skipping dinner?"

Honestly, right then she would have happily agreed to stripping naked and making love on the floor. But all she said was, "I'd feel just fine about that."

His grin suggested that he knew the full extent of what she'd left unsaid. "I'm taking you upstairs now. You might want to move the sauce to the fridge. Because I intend to keep you occupied for a very long time."

"That sounds like heaven to me." She put the lid on, then slipped the pot into the fridge. She started to turn back to him, but ended up squealing when he hoisted her up and tossed her over his shoulder. "You nut! Put me down. If you hurt yourself so you can't make love to me, I'm going to be so irritated."

"Not happening," he said, settling her gently on the bed and going to work on her clothes. "Besides, I'd be more than happy to make love to you even if I was in traction."

She snorted, then peeled her jeans the rest of the way off and leaned over to start unbuttoning his. "Very romantic."

"Everything with you is romantic."

She sighed, not willing to make a joke out of that, because she felt exactly the same way.

He straddled her, his already hard erection rubbing enticingly over her belly as he bent forward then gently teased each of her breasts with his fingers before lowering his mouth to suck and lick and tease and tickle.

She squirmed beneath him, her heart pounding, her inner thighs already slick with need. "Please, Parker. Don't wait. I want it fast—we can take our time after. But right now, I just need to feel you inside me."

He met her eyes, his full of desire. "Baby, I

wouldn't dream of making you wait. Slowly, deliciously slowly, he eased down her body. Then he shifted so that he was on his knees and he lifted her hips, drawing her up so that his cock teased her center and her legs were spread wide. The position felt wicked and a little wild, but the moment he drew her close, his body thrusting forward as he eased inside of her, she knew this was going to be a new route to heaven.

He took her that way at first. Filling her so deliciously. And then, as she trembled, he shifted so that his body was hard and heavy above her. Faster and deeper he thrust inside her, and she urged him on, her fingers tight around his neck, her nails digging into him as she rose higher and higher, her body spinning out, losing touch, coming close to the sweet explosion.

"Parker. I'm close. Oh, please."

"Come with me, baby," he demanded, his hand reaching between their bodies to tease her clit and edge her the final way over, so that they exploded together, wild and hot and sweaty and sated.

When she had her wits back, she breathed in deep, her mind in a muddle, her body so deliciously satisfied. "You're amazing," she said, and he murmured the same back to her, then held her close as she ran a finger lightly over his chest until he finally put his hand over hers and simply pressed it close. "Stop that," he said, laughing. "It tickles."

"Punishment for all you did to me. Some of that tickled, too."

"Oh, did it?" He rolled over, pinning her down. "I think I just might have to tickle you a bit more."

She squealed, but the sound was cut off by his kiss—and then by the way his stomach growled.

He looked at her, his expression sheepish. "I guess it might be time for that spaghetti."

"I guess so." Laughing, she got out of bed, then pulled on the yoga pants and tank top that were hanging over the back of the recliner by the window.

She peeked outside once she was dressed, then frowned. "It's there again."

"What is?" he asked, coming to her side once he'd pulled his jeans on.

"I keep seeing this black car." She grimaced. "It's making me paranoid. When I left LA —never mind."

He rested his hand on her shoulder. "Tell me."

"There was a car in LA," she admitted. "And other stuff, too." She felt the tightness in her chest as she began to talk. "I'm sure it was Carlton, though I couldn't ever prove it."

"I'm sure you're right," he said. "But what makes you think so."

She frowned, wondering what made Parker so sure, but filed it away to ask later. So far, she hadn't told him about what happened in LA, and right then it seemed terribly important to get it off her chest.

"We dated for about four months," she began, and Parker nodded.

"I remember when you got together. I asked you out right after you two started dating. You were sweet about it, but told me that even though you and Carlton had just started going out, that you weren't comfortable seeing two men at the same time."

"You suggested I dump him and go out with you," she recalled, then sighed. "Boy, do I wish I had."

He took her hand. "Water under the bridge. Tell me the rest."

She drew a breath. "At first it was okay. But in the weeks before I finally broke up with him, he got weird. Creepy weird."

"How?"

"He used to drive by my apartment at night, then he'd call to ask where I was if he didn't see my car." She sat on the edge of the bed. "He'd interrogate me. Ask me what I'd been doing and who I was with. And about the same time, he started sending me specific clothes—saying I needed to wear one thing or another to a party or on a date, and then getting irritated if I said I'd planned something else."

She lifted a shoulder. "There was other weird stuff, but that started the ball rolling, and I broke up with him."

"I remember when you did. I suspected the reason was something like that, although since he never seemed your type, I thought that might have been why you broke up."

She cocked her head, studying him. "I didn't realize you were paying attention. Especially since I'd turned you down."

He pulled on his shirt. "I told you in New Orleans—I was attracted to you long before I actually asked you out. So it always irked me that Carlton had what I wanted." His head emerged, and he smiled at her. "But now I win," he teased, making her laugh as he sat beside her on the bed.

"Seriously, there was a group of us who went

out for drinks about once a week. Carlton talked the most about who he was dating and what was going on. He didn't talk much while you were together, but once you broke up … well, let's just say his ego was sorely bruised."

"Jerk," she said. "He started stalking my house. I can't prove it, but I know it was him. I'd see a black sedan, and then it would disappear. And calls from blocked numbers. And flowers sent without any card that would say creepy things. One said *You look beautiful in your pale blue nightie.* But I'd never worn that for him. I bought it as a break-up present to myself. Which meant he had to have been looking through my window."

She shivered, and he wrapped his arms around her, keeping her warm. "I'm so sorry," he said. "Do you think the car you just saw out the window has something to do with Carlton?"

"No. Yes. I don't know." She closed her hands over his at the waist. "It's just a black car. I see them pretty much everywhere. I think it's just a trigger, you know. Something that calls it all back and makes me fear I'm not done with Carlton."

"You are," he said fiercely. "You know if that bastard came back, I'd protect you."

She smiled up at him. "My hero."

He kissed the top of her head. "I look after what's mine."

She turned in his arms. "Am I?"

"What?"

"Am I yours?"

"Oh, baby, yes." He started to kiss her again, then paused, his attention drawn to the window. "Look," he said, as a spry elderly woman with a cane approached the car. The driver emerged, opened the back door for her, and when the woman was settled, he got back in and the car took off.

She caught Parker's eye, then laughed. "Well, I promise I wasn't imagining the things that happened in LA. It was—well, there was more of it." She drew in a breath. "It's why I left like that. My sister stayed way too long with an abusive, paranoid, stalking asshole. And that wasn't a mistake I was willing to make."

"I'm glad you left," he said. "Carlton was obsessed. He might have gotten tired and stopped. But he might have hurt you, too."

She frowned. "It sounds like you know what you're talking about."

"I do. He told me. Or some of it."

She gaped at him. "*What?*"

He rubbed his fingers to his temples, then

turned away from her. "One night after the others left, he told me how pissed he was. How you'd humiliated him. How he was going to make you pay. I told him he was being an ass. That he needed to put you in the past and move on, and that you don't stalk ex-girlfriends. I don't remember exactly what he said, but it was clear he'd already started harassing you, and that he was going to make it worse. Was going to start talking smack about you to your clients, that kind of thing."

"Good God." She felt cold, and any doubts she'd had about leaving LA faded. "I never—I don't think he did. I stay in touch with Kasey, and she would have told me."

"I convinced him not to."

"You did? How?"

His eyes were flat, his expression stone. "I beat the shit out of him, honestly. And I told him if he did anything more to you—anything at all—I'd finish the job."

"Parker…"

"Maybe I shouldn't have, but Christ, the things he talked about doing to you. I just—"

She cut him off, taking his hand in hers, then sliding into his arms. "Thank you," she whispered, then captured his mouth with a long, slow kiss.

When she broke away, she met his eyes, her body shimmering with desire. "I don't think we're going to manage dinner at all," she said, taking his hand and leading her back to the bed. "Right now, all I'm hungry for is you."

Chapter Twelve

"FASTER," Megan ordered as Parker whipped in and out of traffic. "I don't want to be late for the shoot. And neither do you."

Even though The Fix had rented a van, Megan had texted Eva last night to say that she was going to visit the various locations on her own. If it turned out they'd forgotten anything needed for any of the shoots, she could make a quick run to the store.

And she'd casually mentioned that Parker would ride with her. Just to keep her company, of course.

Uh-huh, Eva had texted back. *You do that.*

The fact was, Megan's role at the shoot was minimal. Most of the guys wouldn't need makeup, and even blemishes didn't need to be covered—not that these six guys had any—because Eva could take care of it during editing.

Still, Parker had to be there for the whole thing, and so Megan was coming not just as the makeup artist, but also as the general gopher for the shoot.

A shoot they were going to be late for. Because of sex.

She grinned at the thought.

"What?" Parker asked, shooting a glance at her.

"Eyes on the road," she ordered. They were in his Ferrari, her make-up case practically filling the tiny trunk. "And I was thinking what a wanton woman I've become. Almost late for work because I overslept, exhausted from the lingering effects of too much sex."

"Hmm. Well, I suppose we could cut back…"

"Do not even tease me about that," she said sternly, making him laugh.

They drove for a few more minutes as she mentally ran through the plan for the day. It was going to be a long one. She frowned, then turned to him with a sudden thought. "Hey, your sister doesn't live in town, does she? Is her home in Houston?"

His laugh held no humor. "No. When she walked away from the family, she moved to Connecticut. She's married now with a husband

and daughter and a big old house they always seem to be restoring."

"So I did totally monopolize your time with her. I'm so sorry. And now you don't get to see her today either?" She couldn't believe she'd been so thoughtless.

He reached over and took her hand, squeezing it before taking hold of the wheel again. "You're sweet to think about it, but no. She was only in town for the day to pick up some trial packets."

Megan made a whooshing motion over her head.

"That's right. I haven't told you." He glanced at her, flashing a smile. "I think about telling you so much that I forget what we haven't talked about."

The meaning of those words filled her with joy, and she sighed happily as she told him to go ahead and tell her right then.

"Did you pay attention to the list of charities we made for the Mr. June contest?"

She shook her head. "Probably should have, what with my job and all. But I've been a little distracted."

"My donation went to the International Center for the Treatment and Study of Autism. I'm no longer on the board, but five years ago, I was one of the founding members."

She stayed quiet, anticipating where he was going, but not wanting to interrupt.

"Becky—my sister—well, her daughter is autistic. Severely so."

"What's her name?"

"Cecily," he said, his face lighting up. "She's my only niece, so maybe I'm biased. But I'm pretty sure she's the most adorable little girl on the planet. She's eight now. Diagnosed at three. And she's one of the reasons I founded PCM. We manufacture a wide range of pharmaceuticals, but most of our R&D goes to autism. And Cecily is in all the trials. Right now, we're testing a topical treatment, and although the data hasn't been fully analyzed, based on Becky's anecdotal evidence, I think we may have found something."

"A cure?"

He shook his head. "No. But a treatment. And that's something."

She reached over and pressed her hand to his thigh. "I had no idea. I'm sorry about Cecily, but I'm so glad she has an uncle like you. And I'm sorry I didn't get to meet Becky."

He took his eyes off the road long enough to

meet her eyes. "I promise," he said, his voice heavy
with meaning. "You will."

They drove in silence the rest of the way, until
he turned off the highway and maneuvered his way
over surface streets to finally park in front of Amy's
Ice Cream in the Arboretum parking lot.

A high end outdoor shopping center, the
Arboretum had become popular with everyone
from little kids to high schoolers to college students
not only because of its variety of stores and restaurants, but because of the carved stone cows that
dominated a grassy area near the center of the
property.

They found the rest of the group already there,
with Eva walking around the cows as Reece—Mr.
January—sat atop one, his shirt off and his incredible tats gleaming in the morning sunlight that
came dappled through the trees.

That's why they were starting here; Eva wanted
the effect of the light piercing the canopy of leaves.
Sunset would be for the shot at the bridge.

"That's good," Eva was saying as Parker and
Megan stepped beside Spencer and Brooke. "Just
lean forward a bit." Spencer had won the title of
Mr. February and was the co-star of *The Business
Plan* with Brooke.

"I never would have thought straddling a cow could be hot," Mina said, coming over with Cameron, who was Mr. March. "But I gotta admit it works."

"We should have it on video," Brooke added, shooting Megan a grin. "Those things are slippery. You should have seen the trouble Reece had getting on."

She laughed, but Parker just said, "Great," then went to take a seat on blanket someone had spread on the grass. Tyree was already there, his chin perched on his fist as he watched Eva work. He might be Mr. May, but Megan was certain he would have come even if he wasn't taking a turn in front of the camera. And as for Mr. April, Nolan, the local drive time DJ was sprawled on the blanket, eyes closed, with headphones tight on his ears.

When Eva finished with Reece and called Spencer up to the cows, Brooke sidled closer to Megan. "I keep wanting to talk to you, but every time I see you Parker is right there next to you."

A niggle of worry tugged at Megan, but she shoved it down. "What about?"

Brooke laughed. "Nothing bad," she said, apparently hearing the trepidation in Megan's voice. "It's just that I went to high school with

Parker. So I saw him for years, you know? But I've never seen him lit up like this." Her smile widened. "You must have really gotten under his skin."

Megan sighed happily, appreciating the woman's words. "I don't know about that," she said, glancing sideways to where Parker sat chatting with Tyree. "But he definitely got under mine."

Chapter Thirteen

"I CAN'T BELIEVE you're just blithely abandoning me," Parker said, tugging her fingers lightly as if to draw her back into bed.

"Too bad for you," she said, pulling her hand free, then laughing as she danced backward out of his reach. "I mean, I can only spend so much time with my boy toy."

"Mmm. I think I like the sound of that." He twined his hands behind his head as he sat up, then he reached over and pressed the button for the electronic drape, flooding the penthouse condo with light. "Hop back in bed and play with me some more."

She let her eyes roam appreciatively over his truly exceptional bare chest that she'd come to know so intimately. Her gaze dipped lower to the sheet that covered the rest of him, but was tented enough to prove that he'd been serious about his offer to play.

"Hold that thought," she said, forcing herself not to laugh.

"Why don't you hold it for me?"

The laugh bubbled out. "Perv."

She took a step toward his bathroom. Like everything else in his condo, it was brilliantly appointed and wonderfully luxurious, with the most incredible shower she'd ever seen, complete with a rain-style head above and a series of jets that sprayed from three of the four walls.

She turned back to him. "Although it is a big shower, and I really should clean up before I meet the girls…" She was having breakfast at Magnolia Cafe on Lake Austin Boulevard with Taylor and Mina. Originally, they'd planned to go running, but they'd unanimously agreed that being lazy and catching up on gossip would be much more fun.

"You really should," he said, tossing the sheet aside, and then striding toward her. She glanced down, her pulse kicking up at the sight of his erection, hard and huge.

She swallowed. "Wow. You're really excited about that shower, huh?"

His smile was pure sin. "You have no idea."

She narrowed her eyes as she watched him approach, her own bare skin feeling hot and itchy with anticipation. "Just promise me you won't make me late to meet the girls."

"Cross my heart," he said, then took her hand and led her to the shower.

SHE WAS twelve minutes late for breakfast, and although she swore it was because of traffic, she saw the knowing glint in the other women's eyes.

"You're off the hook," Taylor said, her hair tucked under a BoHo style bandana. "We just got seated. The wait here just gets worse and worse."

"Worth it, though," Mina said. "I'm splurging on gingerbread pancakes." She gave both of them the evil eye in turn. "And we *are* running tomorrow. Otherwise my ass will not survive the way I've been eating lately." She leaned back in the booth, looking smug. "Great sex makes you hungry."

Taylor rolled her eyes. "I don't even want to hear about it. You and Cam. This one and Parker. Honestly, I feel like I'm going to shrivel up and die if I don't get laid soon."

"Don't die," Megan said, squeezing her friend's hand. "Who'd stage manage the contest?"

"Bitch," Taylor said mildly, then smiled sweetly at the waitress who arrived to take their order.

"Speaking of great sex," Mina said after the waitress left, "you're looking chipper this morning." She raised a brow, focusing on Megan. "All brimming over with vim and vigor."

Megan laughed. "I deny nothing. But I'm also not sharing details."

"Totally unfair," Mina said, as Taylor rolled her eyes.

"Vim and vigor?" Taylor glanced toward Mina. "Who talks like that?"

Mina ignored her. "Come on. Tell us everything."

"Oh, great," Megan said. "It's analyze Megan time."

"It's going well, then?"

She sighed, remembering the morning. Heck, remembering all their time together. "I think I'm really falling for him."

"And it's mutual?"

Megan thought of Parker's touch. The way he talked about her struggles to rebuild her business and his support of her ambition to take it further.

She thought of the way they laughed, the heated way he looked at her. The way he'd stood up for her in LA against Carlton. And, mostly, about the way he made her feel safe and loved and special. "Yeah. It really is."

"That's so great."

"I know, right? After the weirdo I dated in LA, I thought…" She trailed off, not wanting to let Carlton-the-prick into her thoughts. "At any rate, let's just say that Austin's been very good to me."

"Excellent," Mina said.

"Talk about reaping the rewards," Taylor added. "First you screw him with the flyer, then you end up getting screwed right back. Only in the best possible way of course."

Megan tossed her napkin at Taylor. "Crude, much?"

"But true," Taylor said.

And since Megan couldn't actually deny it, she only shook her head in mock exasperation.

"Do we want to catch a movie after this?" Taylor asked.

"I'm in," Mina said, but Megan shook her head.

"I need to run by work first, and then I have to do laundry and change the cat boxes."

"You really know how to have a good time," Taylor said.

"It's because she's having a good time that she's avoided all those things," Mina quipped.

Megan laughed, then batted her eyes innocently. "She's not wrong."

"So why are you going into work?" Taylor asked a few minutes later when the waitress delivered their food. "I thought you were off for the next couple of days."

"Technically, I am." She had a few makeup gigs lined up, so she'd pulled back on her schedule at The Fix. "This morning was supposed to be a bridal shoot, but they pushed it back a week—I guess the dress isn't ready. So I thought I'd pop in and run something by Jenna and Tyree."

"Yeah? Tell."

"I was thinking that since Tyree's releasing the cookbook with the calendar later in the year, maybe we should do a big, fancy food fair. The Fix could sponsor it, but we could invite other bars and restaurants. A community building thing, but also great promo. Because the other bars would have flyers at their locations, too, and the flyers would all prominently feature The Fix, what with us being the main sponsor."

Taylor and Mina exchanged glances.

"What?" Megan asked, a little paranoid.

"That's a really great idea," Mina said.

"You'd need to do it someplace other than The Fix." Taylor said. "Neutral territory, you know?"

"Hmm," Megan said. "You're right." She was silent for a minute, then sat up straight. "That guy who Parker introduced me to the night of the Mr. June contest. Darrin or Derek or something. He's some big shot hotel dude."

"There you go. Ask Parker for an introduction."

"I will." She dug into her breakfast, moaning in ecstasy because the gingerbread pancakes really were like a slice of heaven. "But first, I'll make sure Jenna and Tyree like the idea."

Megan was so psyched by the idea that she finished the meal in record time, then actually left her friends before they even got the check, tossing enough cash on the table to cover her share and then some.

She hurried to The Fix, dragged Tyree and Jenna into the office, and was thrilled when they both thought the idea was fabulous.

Giddy, she walked home, planning to ask Parker for an intro that evening.

She was still smiling when she reached her

building. And even the fact that some annoying person had used their bike to prop open the pedestrian gate didn't spoil her mood. But she had to wonder why people went out of their way to make secure properties insecure.

She was slipping inside, when a woman in leggings and a helmet hurried toward her, apologizing as she grabbed the bike. "Forgot my water bottle," she said, then gave Megan a wave as she headed off down the street.

Megan rolled her eyes and started walking the few yards to her front door, only to see someone waiting on the stoop. A man, sitting with his head down as he tapped out something on his phone.

She felt the chill first, even before she recognized him, and she started to back away. But then he looked up, his smile wide and welcoming and utterly charming.

"Megan," Carlton said. "I've been waiting for you."

Chapter Fourteen

TERROR SLUICED OVER MEGAN, and she stood stone still, her blood like ice, her eyes fixed on the man in front of her.

Casually, as if this were no big deal at all, he stood up, then flashed her that brilliant smile that had charmed her so thoroughly the first time they'd met. "Wow, Megan. You look great. Austin agrees with you."

"Get away from me."

His brow furrowed, and he shook his head as if confused. "Hey, whoa. What's wrong?"

"Do not even try to bullshit me. Get the fuck away or I'm calling the cops."

He lifted his hands in surrender. "What the hell happened to make you so paranoid?" His eyes widened. "Oh, shit. Is it Parker? Am I too late?"

She opened her mouth to respond, realized she didn't understand what he meant by any of that, then closed it again. "Just go. Dammit, Carlton, just leave me alone, please. Can't you just leave me alone?"

"No, not when I'm scared for you." Sincerity oozed from his voice. "I tried to call, but you blocked my number." He exhaled, then shook his head. "I get cutting ties with an ex, Megan, but that seemed a little extreme."

"Extreme!"

Before she could continue, he barreled on. "But since I was going to be in Austin anyway, I thought I'd warn you in person."

She should tell him again to get lost, and then call the police if he didn't. But, dammit, she wanted to know what he meant. Still, she pulled out her phone, then held it tight, ready to hit the SOS icon if she needed to. "Warn me about what?"

"Parker," he said, the name like a bullet to her heart. "I saw a picture of you with him at some bar, and I just—oh, hell, Megan. I couldn't live with myself if I didn't warn you. Especially after he did all that weird stalking shit in LA."

Her legs went weak and she stumbled backward. "What weird stalking shit?"

"Driving by your house. Calling you. Leaving flowers."

"Bullshit."

"I wish it was. I went to your place one night after we broke up. I had a pink T-shirt of yours I wanted to return."

She remembered the shirt; she never had gotten it back.

"I got distracted when I saw Parker sitting in a car across from your place. I confronted him—he didn't tell me the details, but I put together enough."

She shook her head. "You lying sack of shit."

"And then the son-of-a-bitch cornered me at my house and beat the living shit out of me."

She swallowed. If nothing else, she knew that was true.

"Pretty fucked up, right? They arrested him for assault, but we've been friends for a long time. I figured he just snapped. So I cooperated when he wanted to sweep it under the rug. I mean, he's got the kind of money to make that happen."

He stepped toward her, close, almost pinning her against one of the stone support columns. "You should go. Get the hell out of Austin before he starts his shit all over again. He's scarily obsessed with you, Megan. He has been for a long time. Did you know he used to ask around about you? Wanted to know where you grew up. Stuff like that."

She swallowed, wanting to force out the words. Wanting to tell the bastard in her face that she didn't believe it. *Couldn't* believe it. But the words wouldn't come. She was trapped behind a wall of fear.

"You do know," he said, his tone menacing as he leaned in closer. "I can see on your face that you know exactly what I'm talking about."

"Megan!"

Relief crashed through her as Carlton leapt back. Megan gasped, then turned to find Parker racing toward her, her spare set of keys tight in his hand. He didn't pause, he didn't even stumble. He just slammed his fist into Carlton's face and sent the little bastard crashing to the ground.

"Get inside," he told her.

Her eyes went wide. "What are you going to do?"

He turned to her, his eyes hard on hers. "Do you trust me?"

"Don't do it, Megan," Carlton said. "You don't even have to believe me. Just don't trust him."

She thought of all the horrible things that

Carlton had said to her. Of all the accusations he'd made. Scary things that, if they were true, meant that she'd never seen the real Parker.

She thought of how Parker had intimated that he'd learned about her past recently, but Carlton suggested he'd poked around in LA. If it was true, then why did Parker lie to her? There were valid reasons, yes. But there were also scary ones.

She thought of the truth that Carlton had shared, too, about the fact that Parker had beaten him up. And, somehow, had kept it out of the papers and the courts.

Then she looked into Parker's eyes, and she thought about the truth she knew in her heart. The man that she knew. That she'd seen so intimately.

And that settled that.

"Yes," she said. "I trust you absolutely."

Chapter Fifteen

"THANKS, MAN," Parker said to Brent as they watched a local detective haul Carlton's complaining, bitching carcass away.

"Landon will make sure he gets on a plane back to LA," Brent said, "but he's only doing it as a favor to me. We can't really press charges for today. After all, you're the one who slugged him."

"I don't want him coming back," Parker said. His mind was still reeling from the horror of knowing that it was only serendipity that he'd been there at the right time. "I don't want him ever getting close to Megan again."

"I've got an idea about that," the ex-cop said. "I said we can't press charges for today. But maybe the cops in LA can latch onto something from the past."

"I'm listening."

"You said you used to walk in the same circle as that piece of shit. How many women other than Megan do you think he harassed?"

"I don't know. A lot, I'd guess."

"So we talk to them. Get an investigator to do the leg work, then take the package to the cops, all wrapped up with a nice, shiny bow. He might do time. Even if he doesn't, it'll make it a hell of a lot easier to deal with him if he ever sets foot in Austin again."

Parker went rigid. "Do you think he will?"

Brent shook his head. "In my experience, no. That kind of guy wants to stay in control, but only in the shadows. Once the gig's exposed, he has no interest stepping into the light. He's not about revenge. He's about fear and humiliation and control. He knows Megan won't be afraid anymore. She has you."

"She damn sure does."

"But we'll still be careful," Brent said. "Just in case I'm wrong."

Parker nodded. "You have an investigator in mind?"

"I'm friends with a guy who heads up an Austin division of Stark International. He does a lot of security tech work, and he introduced me to the Stark International Security Chief. I figure any security guy who works for Damien Stark knows his shit."

"I'd think so," Parker agreed. He'd never met the billionaire in person, but he knew the man by reputation. "Will this security guy do you a favor?"

"I'm sure of it. Either him or someone else." He gave Parker a friendly clap on the shoulder. "One way or another, we'll nail that bastard's ass to the wall. And we'll make sure he doesn't harass Megan or anyone else again."

"Thanks."

"No problem." He nodded toward Megan's condo. "I'm done here, and I think you have somewhere else to be."

"Yes, I do," Parker said, then moved to the door. He opened it, and she flew into his arms, relief and trust and love clinging to her like perfume. And right then, he knew without a doubt that this woman was his, now and forever.

And damned if he didn't belong to her, too.

"I'M SO SORRY," Parker said, lifting her into the

safety of his arms as he kicked the door closed, then carried her to the sofa.

"What on earth for?" She sighed and curled against him, and for the first time that evening, the world righted itself.

"For not being here sooner."

"Are you insane? That you came at all was a miracle. You swooped in like a superhero." She'd almost burst into tears when she'd seen him, she'd been so relieved. And now he was apologizing?

"And for letting you think that I looked into your background because of that flyer. That wasn't true. I poked around in LA."

She nodded. "I figured Carlton was right about that."

His brows lifted.

"About the fact," she clarified. "But not about the menace." She twined their fingers together. Maybe she should be angry about the white lie, but she wasn't. "But why did you check me out?"

"I told you. I've wanted you for a long time. What I learned only made me want you more. Fucking Carlton just got there first."

"But you're the one who stuck with me," she said. "My knight in shining armor."

"Maybe not that shiny, but I'll take what I can get."

"You rescued me," she said. "That qualifies for knighthood in my book." She frowned. "Actually, why did you come at all? I didn't think I was going to see you until later tonight."

"I had some news for you. But it can wait."

"Good news?" When he nodded, she snuggled closer. "Well, tell me now. After that encounter, I'm all about the good news."

"Remember in New Orleans how you mentioned that you wanted to take your makeup business to the next level? Get into skincare products?"

"I remember." She'd mentioned it early on, and then they'd talked about it again at length as they walked through the Garden District. She'd told him how she made her own, experimenting to find the best texture and results, but also admitting that since she wasn't a chemist, she could only take her ideas so far. "What about it?"

"I told you about the trial for Cecily, right? The new topical that PCM is working on?"

She nodded, confused.

"Well, I was talking with the folks at the lab, and at least two of my chemists said they'd love to chat with you about what you have in mind. Maybe see about putting together a sample of a product that you could test on your clients and refine."

Her breath caught in her throat, and she thought her heart might swell to breaking. She blinked, and a tear trickled down her cheek. "You did that for me?"

"Baby, I'd do pretty much anything for you. Don't you know that by now?"

The tears fell in earnest. "Yeah? In that case, I think you should make love to me now."

He chuckled, then lightly kissed her. "Happy to oblige."

Gently, he carried her to bed like she was the most precious thing in the world to him. He undressed her, then pulled her to him, and when they kissed, it seemed as if the whole world fell away. It was only the two of them, with the future wide open in front of them, while fear and regrets were left far behind.

"Now," she said as she knelt on the bed, then held out a hand to tug him close. "I want to feel you moving inside me. I want you to take me to the stars, and I want to take you right along with me."

"To the stars? Baby, you take me to heaven every day." He cupped her cheek, and she fell back against the pillows, drawing him down, over her. Into her.

She arched up as he thrust deep inside, filling her with his body and his love. And when passion cut through him, making him tremble, she held him close and followed him over, shattering into a million pieces, but unafraid. Because she knew that Parker would always be there to put her back together again.

When the electricity in her limbs finally calmed and she could breathe again, she snuggled closer, then sighed. "You're mine, Parker Manning." She propped herself up on her elbow. "Just so you know, I'm not ever letting you get away."

"Good to hear," he said, the love in his eyes making her heart sing. "Because I'm not going anywhere."

Epilogue

The Night of the Mr. June Contest

AMANDA EASED toward the back of the bar, thinking that she'd slip out through the alley exit while the contest was going on. Not that she wanted to miss it, but she definitely had someplace else she wanted to be right now. And though going out the front might make more sense, she didn't want to get waylaid by one of her friends.

Derek.

She sighed with happiness—and with anticipation—as all of her girly parts fired up at the prospect of seeing him again.

For almost a year now, they'd been meeting in secret whenever he came to town for business, usually every month or so. It had started when he'd picked her up on the sidewalk outside The Fix. She'd gone in for nothing more than a drink and to soothe her own crappy mood, but his tempting smile had caught her attention, and his tempting offer had won her over.

They'd been clear from the get-go that the encounter would be nothing more than a fling. She wasn't interested in more, and he swore that neither was he. And when he told her that he was only in town for the night for business, the whole encounter had seemed like a no-brainer.

A fabulously sexy, decadently delicious, orgasm-inducing no-brainer. Seriously, the man had been the best sex of her life, and the glow of satisfaction afterwards had lasted for at least a week.

And the very best part? No strings.

Because the last thing that Amanda wanted or needed was an actual relationship.

Which, in her book, made Derek the absolute perfect man.

She eased through the crowd, her mind on her lingerie drawer, and was just about to slip into the hallway, when she heard the familiar deep voice with the Texas drawl calling her name.

"Amanda."

She turned, her breath leaving her as she saw

him, his broad shoulders filling the space and his eyes full of so much passion she knew that her panties were already soaked. If it wouldn't be so damn dangerous, she'd just drag him into the ladies room and have her way with him right then.

Instead, all she said was, "Hey."

"Meet me in our room in an hour?"

"Absolutely."

"I have news," he said. "I was going to wait to tell you, but baby, I'm too excited."

"Really?" She couldn't imagine what it could be. Maybe tickets to a show tonight?

He took her hand, then leaned in close, his breath tickling her ear. "I'm moving here, sweetheart. No more waiting. From now on, you can have me anytime you want me." He pulled back just enough to meet her eyes. "And baby, I always want you."

Are you eager to learn which Man of the Month book features which sexy hero? Here's a handy list!

Down On Me - meet Reece
Hold On Tight - meet Spencer
Need You Now - meet Cameron
Start Me Up - meet Nolan
Get It On - meet Tyree
In Your Eyes - meet Parker
Turn Me On - meet Derek
Shake It Up - meet Landon
All Night Long - meet Easton
In Too Deep - meet Matthew
Light My Fire - meet Griffin
Walk The Line - meet Brent
&
Bar Bites: A Man of the Month Cookbook

Down On Me excerpt

Did you miss book one in the Man of the Month series? Here's an excerpt from Down On Me!

Chapter One

Reece Walker ran his palms over the slick, soapy ass of the woman in his arms and knew that he was going straight to hell.

Not because he'd slept with a woman he barely knew. Not because he'd enticed her into bed with a series of well-timed bourbons and particularly inventive half-truths. Not even because he'd lied to his best friend Brent about why Reece couldn't drive with him to the airport to pick up Jenna, the third player in their trifecta of lifelong friendship.

No, Reece was staring at the fiery pit because he

was a lame, horny asshole without the balls to tell the naked beauty standing in the shower with him that she wasn't the woman he'd been thinking about for the last four hours.

And if that wasn't one of the pathways to hell, it damn sure ought to be.

He let out a sigh of frustration, and Megan tilted her head, one eyebrow rising in question as she slid her hand down to stroke his cock, which was demonstrating no guilt whatsoever about the whole going to hell issue. "Am I boring you?"

"Hardly." That, at least, was the truth. He felt like a prick, yes. But he was a well-satisfied one. "I was just thinking that you're beautiful."

She smiled, looking both shy and pleased—and Reece felt even more like a heel. What the devil was wrong with him? She *was* beautiful. And hot and funny and easy to talk to. Not to mention good in bed.

But she wasn't Jenna, which was a ridiculous comparison. Because Megan qualified as fair game, whereas Jenna was one of his two best friends. She trusted him. Loved him. And despite the way his cock perked up at the thought of doing all sorts of delicious things with her in bed, Reece knew damn well that would never happen. No way was he risking their friendship. Besides, Jenna didn't love him like that. Never had, never would.

And that—plus about a billion more reasons— meant that Jenna was entirely off-limits.

Too bad his vivid imagination hadn't yet gotten the memo.

Fuck it.

He tightened his grip, squeezing Megan's perfect rear. "Forget the shower," he murmured. "I'm taking you back to bed." He needed this. Wild. Hot. Demanding. And dirty enough to keep him from thinking.

Hell, he'd scorch the earth if that's what it took to burn Jenna from his mind—and he'd leave Megan limp, whimpering, and very, very satisfied. His guilt. Her pleasure. At least it would be a win for one of them.

And who knows? Maybe he'd manage to fuck the fantasies of his best friend right out of his head.

It didn't work.

Reece sprawled on his back, eyes closed, as Megan's gentle fingers traced the intricate outline of the tattoos inked across his pecs and down his arms. Her touch was warm and tender, in stark contrast to the way he'd just fucked her—a little too wild, a little too hard, as if he were fighting a battle, not making love.

Well, that was true, wasn't it?

But it was a battle he'd lost. Victory would have brought oblivion. Yet here he was, a naked woman beside him, and his thoughts still on Jenna, as wild and intense and impossible as they'd been since that night eight months ago when the earth had shifted beneath him, and he'd let himself look at her as a woman and not as a friend.

One breathtaking, transformative night, and Jenna didn't even realize it. And he'd be damned if he'd ever let her figure it out.

Beside him, Megan continued her exploration, one fingertip tracing the outline of a star. "No names? No wife or girlfriend's initials hidden in the design?"

He turned his head sharply, and she burst out laughing.

"Oh, don't look at me like that." She pulled the sheet up to cover her breasts as she rose to her knees beside him. "I'm just making conversation. No hidden agenda at all. Believe me, the last thing I'm interested in is a relationship." She scooted away, then sat on the edge of the bed, giving him an enticing view of her bare back. "I don't even do overnights."

As if to prove her point, she bent over, grabbed her bra off the floor, and started getting dressed.

"Then that's one more thing we have in common." He pushed himself up, rested his back against the headboard, and enjoyed the view as she wiggled into her jeans.

"Good," she said, with such force that he knew she meant it, and for a moment he wondered what had soured her on relationships.

As for himself, he hadn't soured so much as fizzled. He'd had a few serious girlfriends over the years, but it never worked out. No matter how good it started, invariably the relationship crumbled. Eventually, he had to acknowledge that he simply wasn't relationship material. But that didn't mean he was a monk, the last eight months notwithstanding.

She put on her blouse and glanced around, then slipped her feet into her shoes. Taking the hint, he got up and pulled on his jeans and T-shirt. "Yes?" he asked, noticing the way she was eying him specu-latively.

"The truth is, I was starting to think you might be in a relationship."

"What? Why?"

She shrugged. "You were so quiet there for a while, I wondered if maybe I'd misjudged you. I thought you might be married and feeling guilty."

Guilty.

The word rattled around in his head, and he groaned. "Yeah, you could say that."

"Oh, *hell*. Seriously?"

"No," he said hurriedly. "Not that. I'm not cheating on my non-existent wife. I wouldn't. Not ever." Not in small part because Reece wouldn't ever have a wife since he thought the institution of marriage was a crock, but he didn't see the need to explain that to Megan.

"But as for guilt?" he continued. "Yeah, tonight I've got that in spades."

She relaxed slightly. "Hmm. Well, sorry about the guilt, but I'm glad about the rest. I have rules, and I consider myself a good judge of character. It makes me cranky when I'm wrong."

"Wouldn't want to make you cranky."

"Oh, you really wouldn't. I can be a total bitch." She sat on the edge of the bed and watched as he tugged on his boots. "But if you're not hiding a wife in your attic, what are you feeling guilty about? I assure you, if it has anything to do with my satisfaction, you needn't feel guilty at all." She flashed a mischievous grin, and he couldn't help but smile back. He hadn't invited a woman into his bed for eight long months. At least he'd had the good fortune to pick one he actually liked.

"It's just that I'm a crappy friend," he admitted.

"I doubt that's true."

"Oh, it is," he assured her as he tucked his wallet into his back pocket. The irony, of course, was that as far as Jenna knew, he was an excellent friend. The best. One of her two pseudo-brothers with whom she'd sworn a blood oath the summer after sixth grade, almost twenty years ago.

From Jenna's perspective, Reece was at least as good as Brent, even if the latter scored bonus points because he was picking Jenna up at the airport while Reece was trying to fuck his personal demons into oblivion. Trying anything, in fact, that would exorcise the memory of how she'd clung to him that night, her curves enticing and her breath intoxicating, and not just because of the scent of too much alcohol.

She'd trusted him to be the white knight, her noble rescuer, and all he'd been able to think about was the feel of her body, soft and warm against his, as he carried her up the stairs to her apartment.

A wild craving had hit him that night, like a tidal wave of emotion crashing over him, washing away the outer shell of friendship and leaving nothing but raw desire and a longing so potent it nearly brought him to his knees.

It had taken all his strength to keep his distance when the only thing he'd wanted was to cover every inch of her naked body with kisses. To stroke her skin and watch her writhe with pleasure.

He'd won a hard-fought battle when he reined in his desire that night. But his victory wasn't without its wounds. She'd pierced his heart when she'd drifted to sleep in his arms, whispering that she loved him—and he knew that she meant it only as a friend.

More than that, he knew that he was the biggest asshole to ever walk the earth.

Thankfully, Jenna remembered nothing of that night. The liquor had stolen her memories, leaving her with a monster hangover, and him with a Jenna-shaped hole in his heart.

"Well?" Megan pressed. "Are you going to tell me? Or do I have to guess?"

"I blew off a friend."

"Yeah? That probably won't score you points in the Friend of the Year competition, but it doesn't sound too dire. Unless you were the best man and blew off the wedding? Left someone stranded at the side of the road somewhere in West Texas? Or promised to feed their cat and totally forgot? Oh, God. Please tell me you didn't kill Fluffy."

He bit back a laugh, feeling slightly better. "A friend came in tonight, and I feel like a complete shit for not meeting her plane."

"Well, there are taxis. And I assume she's an adult?"

"She is, and another friend is there to pick her up."

"I see," she said, and the way she slowly nodded suggested that she saw too much. "I'm guessing that *friend* means *girlfriend*? Or, no. You wouldn't do that. So she must be an ex."

"Really not," he assured her. "Just a friend. Life-long, since sixth grade."

"Oh, I get it. Longtime friend. High expecta-tions. She's going to be pissed."

"Nah. She's cool. Besides, she knows I usually work nights."

"Then what's the problem?"

He ran his hand over his shaved head, the bristles from the day's growth like sandpaper against his palm. "Hell if I know," he lied, then forced a smile, because whether his problem was guilt or lust or just plain stupidity, she hardly deserved to be on the receiving end of his bullshit.

He rattled his car keys. "How about I buy you one last drink before I take you home?"

———

"You're sure you don't mind a working drink?" Reece asked as he helped Megan out of his cherished baby blue vintage Chevy pickup. "Normally I wouldn't take you to my job, but we just hired a new bar back, and I want to see how it's going."

He'd snagged one of the coveted parking spots on Sixth Street, about a block down from The Fix, and he glanced automatically toward the bar, the glow from the windows relaxing him. He didn't own the place, but it was like a second home to him and had been for one hell of a long time.

"There's a new guy in training, and you're not there? I thought you told me you were the manager?"

"I did, and I am, but Tyree's there. The owner, I mean. He's always on site when someone new is starting. Says it's his job, not mine. Besides, Sunday's my day off, and Tyree's a stickler for keeping to the schedule."

"Okay, but why are you going then?"

"Honestly? The new guy's my cousin. He'll probably give me shit for checking in on him, but old habits die hard." Michael had been almost four when Vincent died, and the loss of his dad hit him hard. At sixteen, Reece had tried to be stoic, but Uncle Vincent had been like a second father to him, and he'd always thought of Mike as more brother than cousin. Either way, from that day on, he'd made it his job to watch out for the kid.

"Nah, he'll appreciate it," Megan said. "I've got a little sister, and she gripes when I check up on her, but it's all for show. She likes knowing I have her back. And as for getting a drink where you work, I don't mind at all."

As a general rule, late nights on Sunday were dead, both in the bar and on Sixth Street, the popular downtown Austin street that had been a focal point of the city's nightlife for decades. Tonight was no exception. At half-past one in the morning, the street was mostly deserted. Just a few cars moving slowly, their headlights shining toward the west, and a smattering of couples, stumbling and laughing. Probably tourists on their way back to one of the downtown hotels.

It was late April, though, and the spring weather was drawing both locals and tourists. Soon, the area—and the bar—would be bursting at the seams. Even on a slow Sunday night.

Situated just a few blocks down from Congress Avenue, the main downtown artery, The Fix on Sixth attracted a healthy mix of tourists and locals. The bar had existed in one form or another for decades, becoming a local staple, albeit one that had been falling deeper and deeper into disrepair until Tyree had bought the place six years ago and started it on much-needed life support.

"You've never been here before?" Reece asked as he paused in front of the oak and glass doors etched with the bar's familiar logo.

"I only moved downtown last month. I was in Los Angeles before."

The words hit Reece with unexpected force. Jenna had been in LA, and a wave of both longing and regret crashed over him. He should have gone with Brent. What the hell kind of friend was he, punishing Jenna because he couldn't control his own damn libido?

With effort, he forced the thoughts back. He'd

already beaten that horse to death.

"Come on," he said, sliding one arm around her shoulder and pulling open the door with his other. "You're going to love it."

He led her inside, breathing in the familiar mix of alcohol, southern cooking, and something indiscernible he liked to think of as the scent of a damn good time. As he expected, the place was mostly empty. There was no live music on Sunday nights, and at less than an hour to closing, there were only three customers in the front room.

"Megan, meet Cameron," Reece said, pulling out a stool for her as he nodded to the bartender in introduction. Down the bar, he saw Griffin Draper, a regular, lift his head, his face obscured by his hoodie, but his attention on Megan as she chatted with Cam about the house wines.

Reece nodded hello, but Griffin turned back to his notebook so smoothly and nonchalantly that Reece wondered if maybe he'd just been staring into space, thinking, and hadn't seen Reece or Megan at all. That was probably the case, actually. Griff wrote a popular podcast that had been turned into an even more popular web series, and when he wasn't recording the dialogue, he was usually writing a script.

"So where's Mike? With Tyree?"

Cameron made a face, looking younger than his twenty-four years. "Tyree's gone."

"You're kidding. Did something happen with Mike?" His cousin was a responsible kid. Surely he hadn't somehow screwed up his first day on the job.

"No, Mike's great." Cam slid a Scotch in front of Reece. "Sharp, quick, hard worker. He went off the clock about an hour ago, though. So you just missed him."

"Tyree shortened his shift?"

Cam shrugged. "Guess so. Was he supposed to be on until closing?"

"Yeah." Reece frowned. "He was. Tyree say why he cut him loose?"

"No, but don't sweat it. Your cousin's fitting right in. Probably just because it's Sunday and slow. " He made a face. "And since Tyree followed him out, guess who's closing for the first time alone."

"So you're in the hot seat, huh? " Reece tried to sound casual. He was standing behind Megan's stool, but now he moved to lean against the bar, hoping his casual posture suggested that he wasn't worried at all. He was, but he didn't want Cam to realize it. Tyree didn't leave employees to close on their own. Not until he'd spent weeks training them.

"I told him I want the weekend assistant manager position. I'm guessing this is his way of seeing how I work under pressure."

"Probably," Reece agreed half-heartedly. "What did he say?"

"Honestly, not much. He took a call in the office, told Mike he could head home, then about fifteen minutes later said he needed to take off, too, and that I was the man for the night."

"Trouble?" Megan asked.

"No. Just chatting up my boy," Reece said, surprised at how casual his voice sounded. Because the scenario had trouble printed all over it. He just wasn't sure what kind of trouble.

He focused again on Cam. "What about the waitstaff?" Normally, Tiffany would be in the main bar taking care of the customers who sat at tables. "He didn't send them home, too, did he?"

"Oh, no," Cam said. "Tiffany and Aly are scheduled to be on until closing, and they're in the back with—"

But his last words were drowned out by a high-pitched squeal of "*You're here!*" and Reece looked up to find Jenna Montgomery—the woman he craved —barreling across the room and flinging herself into his arms.

Meet Damien Stark

Only his passion could set her free...

Release Me
Claim Me
Complete Me
Anchor Me
Lost With Me

Meet Damien Stark in Release Me, *book 1 of the wildly sensual series that's left millions of readers breathless ...*

Chapter One

A cool ocean breeze caresses my bare shoulders, and I shiver, wishing I'd taken my roommate's advice and brought a shawl with me tonight. I arrived in Los Angeles only four days ago, and I haven't yet adjusted to the concept of summer temperatures changing with the setting of the sun. In Dallas, June is hot, July is hotter, and August is hell.

Not so in California, at least not by the beach. LA Lesson Number One: Always carry a sweater if you'll be out after dark.

Of course, I could leave the balcony and go back inside to the party. Mingle with the millionaires. Chat up the celebrities. Gaze dutifully at the paintings. It is a gala art opening, after all, and my boss brought me here to meet and greet and charm and chat. Not to lust over the panorama that is coming alive in front of me. Bloodred clouds bursting against the pale orange sky. Blue-gray waves shimmering with dappled gold.

I press my hands against the balcony rail and lean forward, drawn to the intense, unreachable beauty of the setting sun. I regret that I didn't bring the battered Nikon I've had since high school. Not that it would have fit in my itty-bitty beaded purse. And a bulky camera bag paired with a little black dress is a big, fat fashion no-no.

But this is my very first Pacific Ocean sunset,

and I'm determined to document the moment. I pull out my iPhone and snap a picture.

"Almost makes the paintings inside seem redundant, doesn't it?" I recognize the throaty, feminine voice and turn to face Evelyn Dodge, retired actress turned agent turned patron of the arts—and my hostess for the evening.

"I'm so sorry. I know I must look like a giddy tourist, but we don't have sunsets like this in Dallas."

"Don't apologize," she says. "I pay for that view every month when I write the mortgage check. It damn well better be spectacular."

I laugh, immediately more at ease.

"Hiding out?"

"Excuse me?"

"You're Carl's new assistant, right?" she asks, referring to my boss of three days.

"Nikki Fairchild."

"I remember now. Nikki from Texas." She looks me up and down, and I wonder if she's disappointed that I don't have big hair and cowboy boots. "So who does he want you to charm?"

"Charm?" I repeat, as if I don't know exactly what she means.

She cocks a single brow. "Honey, the man would

rather walk on burning coals than come to an art show. He's fishing for investors and you're the bait." She makes a rough noise in the back of her throat. "Don't worry. I won't press you to tell me who. And I don't blame you for hiding out. Carl's brilliant, but he's a bit of a prick."

"It's the brilliant part I signed on for," I say, and she barks out a laugh.

The truth is that she's right about me being the bait. "Wear a cocktail dress," Carl had said. "Something flirty."

Seriously? I mean, *Seriously?*

I should have told him to wear his own damn cocktail dress. But I didn't. Because I want this job. I fought to get this job. Carl's company, C-Squared Technologies, successfully launched three web-based products in the last eighteen months. That track record had caught the industry's eye, and Carl had been hailed as a man to watch.

More important from my perspective, that meant he was a man to learn from, and I'd prepared for the job interview with an intensity bordering on obsession. Landing the position had been a huge coup for me. So what if he wanted me to wear something flirty? It was a small price to pay.

Shit.

"I need to get back to being the bait," I say.

"Oh, hell. Now I've gone and made you feel either guilty or self-conscious. Don't be. Let them get liquored up in there first. You catch more flies with alcohol anyway. Trust me. I know."

She's holding a pack of cigarettes, and now she taps one out, then extends the pack to me. I shake my head. I love the smell of tobacco—it reminds me of my grandfather—but actually inhaling the smoke does nothing for me.

"I'm too old and set in my ways to quit," she says. "But God forbid I smoke in my own damn house. I swear, the mob would burn me in effigy. You're not going to start lecturing me on the dangers of secondhand smoke, are you?"

"No," I promise.

"Then how about a light?"

I hold up the itty-bitty purse. "One lipstick, a credit card, my driver's license, and my phone."

"No condom?"

"I didn't think it was that kind of party," I say dryly.

"I knew I liked you." She glances around the balcony. "What the hell kind of party am I throwing if I don't even have one goddamn candle on one goddamn table? Well, fuck it." She puts the unlit cigarette to her mouth and inhales, her eyes closed and her expression rapturous. I can't help but like her. She wears hardly any makeup, in stark contrast to all the other women here tonight, myself included, and her dress is more of a caftan, the batik pattern as interesting as the woman herself.

She's what my mother would call a brassy broad —loud, large, opinionated, and self-confident. My mother would hate her. I think she's awesome.

She drops the unlit cigarette onto the tile and grinds it with the toe of her shoe. Then she signals to one of the catering staff, a girl dressed all in black and carrying a tray of champagne glasses.

The girl fumbles for a minute with the sliding door that opens onto the balcony, and I imagine those flutes tumbling off, breaking against the hard tile, the scattered shards glittering like a wash of diamonds.

I picture myself bending to snatch up a broken stem. I see the raw edge cutting into the soft flesh at the base of my thumb as I squeeze. I watch myself clutching it tighter, drawing strength from the pain, the way some people might try to extract luck from a rabbit's foot.

The fantasy blurs with memory, jarring me with its potency. It's fast and powerful, and a little disturbing because I haven't needed the pain in a long time, and I don't understand why I'm thinking about it now, when I feel steady and in control.

I am fine, I think. *I am fine, I am fine, I am fine.*

"Take one, honey," Evelyn says easily, holding a flute out to me.

I hesitate, searching her face for signs that my mask has slipped and she's caught a glimpse of my rawness. But her face is clear and genial.

"No, don't you argue," she adds, misinterpreting my hesitation. "I bought a dozen cases and I hate to see good alcohol go to waste. Hell no," she adds when the girl tries to hand her a flute. "I hate the stuff. Get me a vodka. Straight up. Chilled. Four olives. Hurry up, now. Do you want me to dry up like a leaf and float away?"

The girl shakes her head, looking a bit like a twitchy, frightened rabbit. Possibly one that had sacrificed his foot for someone else's good luck.

Evelyn's attention returns to me. "So how do you like LA? What have you seen? Where have you been? Have you bought a map of the stars yet? Dear God, tell me you're not getting sucked into all that tourist bullshit."

"Mostly I've seen miles of freeway and the inside of my apartment."

"Well, that's just sad. Makes me even more glad that Carl dragged your skinny ass all the way out here tonight."

I've put on fifteen welcome pounds since the years when my mother monitored every tiny thing that went in my mouth, and while I'm perfectly happy with my size-eight ass, I wouldn't describe it as skinny. I know Evelyn means it as a compliment, though, and so I smile. "I'm glad he brought me, too. The paintings really are amazing."

"Now don't do that—don't you go sliding into the polite-conversation routine. No, no," she says before I can protest. "I'm sure you mean it. Hell, the paintings are wonderful. But you're getting the flat-eyed look of a girl on her best behavior, and we can't have that. Not when I was getting to know the real you."

"Sorry," I say. "I swear I'm not fading away on you."

Because I genuinely like her, I don't tell her that she's wrong—she hasn't met the real Nikki Fairchild. She's met Social Nikki who, much like Malibu Barbie, comes with a complete set of accessories. In my case, it's not a bikini and a convertible. Instead, I have the *Elizabeth Fairchild Guide for Social Gatherings*.

My mother's big on rules. She claims it's her Southern upbringing. In my weaker moments, I agree. Mostly, I just think she's a controlling bitch. Since the first time she took me for tea at the Mansion at Turtle Creek in Dallas at age three, I have had the rules drilled into my head. How to walk, how to talk, how to dress. What to eat, how much to drink, what kinds of jokes to tell.

I have it all down, every trick, every nuance, and I wear my practiced pageant smile like armor against the world. The result being that I don't think I could truly be myself at a party even if my life depended on it.

This, however, is not something Evelyn needs to know.

"Where exactly are you living?" she asks.

"Studio City. I'm sharing a condo with my best friend from high school."

"Straight down the 101 for work and then back home again. No wonder you've only seen concrete. Didn't anyone tell you that you should have taken an apartment on the Westside?"

"Too pricey to go it alone," I admit, and I can tell that my admission surprises her. When I make the effort—like when I'm Social Nikki—I can't help but look like I come from money. Probably because

I do. Come from it, that is. But that doesn't mean I brought it with me.

"How old are you?"

"Twenty-four."

Evelyn nods sagely, as if my age reveals some secret about me. "You'll be wanting a place of your own soon enough. You call me when you do and we'll find you someplace with a view. Not as good as this one, of course, but we can manage something better than a freeway on-ramp."

"It's not that bad, I promise."

"Of course it's not," she says in a tone that says the exact opposite. "As for views," she continues, gesturing toward the now-dark ocean and the sky that's starting to bloom with stars, "you're welcome to come back anytime and share mine."

"I might take you up on that," I admit. "I'd love to bring a decent camera back here and take a shot or two."

"It's an open invitation. I'll provide the wine and you can provide the entertainment. A young woman loose in the city. Will it be a drama? A rom-com? Not a tragedy, I hope. I love a good cry as much as the next woman, but I like you. You need a happy ending."

I tense, but Evelyn doesn't know she's hit a

nerve. That's why I moved to LA, after all. New life. New story. New Nikki.

I ramp up the Social Nikki smile and lift my champagne flute. "To happy endings. And to this amazing party. I think I've kept you from it long enough."

"Bullshit," she says. "I'm the one monopolizing you, and we both know it."

We slip back inside, the buzz of alcohol-fueled conversation replacing the soft calm of the ocean.

"The truth is, I'm a terrible hostess. I do what I want, talk to whoever I want, and if my guests feel slighted they can damn well deal with it."

I gape. I can almost hear my mother's cries of horror all the way from Dallas.

"Besides," she continues, "this party isn't supposed to be about me. I put together this little shindig to introduce Blaine and his art to the community. He's the one who should be doing the mingling, not me. I may be fucking him, but I'm not going to baby him."

Evelyn has completely destroyed my image of how a hostess for the not-to-be-missed social event of the weekend is supposed to behave, and I think I'm a little in love with her for that.

"I haven't met Blaine yet. That's him, right?" I

point to a tall reed of a man. He is bald, but sports a red goatee. I'm pretty sure it's not his natural color. A small crowd hums around him, like bees drawing nectar from a flower. His outfit is certainly as bright as one.

"That's my little center of attention, all right," Evelyn says. "The man of the hour. Talented, isn't he?" Her hand sweeps out to indicate her massive living room. Every wall is covered with paintings. Except for a few benches, whatever furniture was once in the room has been removed and replaced with easels on which more paintings stand.

I suppose technically they are portraits. The models are nudes, but these aren't like anything you would see in a classical art book. There's something edgy about them. Something provocative and raw. I can tell that they are expertly conceived and carried out, and yet they disturb me, as if they reveal more about the person viewing the portrait than about the painter or the model.

As far as I can tell, I'm the only one with that reaction. Certainly the crowd around Blaine is glowing. I can hear the gushing praise from here.

"I picked a winner with that one," Evelyn says. "But let's see. Who do you want to meet? Rip Carrington and Lyle Tarpin? Those two are guaranteed drama, that's for damn sure, and your room-mate will be jealous as hell if you chat them up."

"She will?"

Evelyn's brows arch up. "Rip and Lyle? They've been feuding for weeks." She narrows her eyes at me. "The fiasco about the new season of their sitcom? It's all over the Internet? You really don't know them?"

"Sorry," I say, feeling the need to apologize. "My school schedule was pretty intense. And I'm sure you can imagine what working for Carl is like."

Speaking of …

I glance around, but I don't see my boss anywhere.

"That is one serious gap in your education," Evelyn says. "Culture—and yes, pop culture counts —is just as important as—what did you say you studied?"

"I don't think I mentioned it. But I have a double major in electrical engineering and computer science."

"So you've got brains and beauty. See? That's something else we have in common. Gotta say, though, with an education like that, I don't see why you signed up to be Carl's secretary."

I laugh. "I'm not, I swear. Carl was looking for

someone with tech experience to work with him on the business side of things, and I was looking for a job where I could learn the business side. Get my feet wet. I think he was a little hesitant to hire me at first—my skills definitely lean toward tech—but I convinced him I'm a fast learner."

She peers at me. "I smell ambition."

I lift a shoulder in a casual shrug. "It's Los Angeles. Isn't that what this town is all about?"

"Ha! Carl's lucky he's got you. It'll be interesting to see how long he keeps you. But let's see … who here would intrigue you …?"

She casts about the room, finally pointing to a fifty-something man holding court in a corner. "That's Charles Maynard," she says. "I've known Charlie for years. Intimidating as hell until you get to know him. But it's worth it. His clients are either celebrities with name recognition or power brokers with more money than God. Either way, he's got all the best stories."

"He's a lawyer?"

"With Bender, Twain & McGuire. Very prestigious firm."

"I know," I say, happy to show that I'm not entirely ignorant, despite not knowing Rip or Lyle. "One of my closest friends works for the firm. He started here but he's in their New York office now."

"Well, come on, then, Texas. I'll introduce you." We take one step in that direction, but then Evelyn stops me. Maynard has pulled out his phone, and is shouting instructions at someone. I catch a few well-placed curses and eye Evelyn sideways. She looks unconcerned "He's a pussycat at heart. Trust me, I've worked with him before. Back in my agenting days, we put together more celebrity biopic deals for our clients than I can count. And we fought to keep a few tell-alls off the screen, too." She shakes her head, as if reliving those glory days, then pats my arm. "Still, we'll wait 'til he calms down a bit. In the meantime, though ..."

She trails off, and the corners of her mouth turn down in a frown as she scans the room again. "I don't think he's here yet, but—oh! Yes! Now *there's* someone you should meet. And if you want to talk views, the house he's building has one that makes my view look like, well, like yours." She points toward the entrance hall, but all I see are bobbing heads and haute couture. "He hardly ever accepts invitations, but we go way back," she says.

I still can't see who she's talking about, but then the crowd parts and I see the man in profile. Goose bumps rise on my arms, but I'm not cold. In fact, I'm suddenly very, very warm.

He's tall and so handsome that the word is almost an insult. But it's more than that. It's not his looks, it's his *presence*. He commands the room simply by being in it, and I realize that Evelyn and I aren't the only ones looking at him. The entire crowd has noticed his arrival. He must feel the weight of all those eyes, and yet the attention doesn't faze him at all. He smiles at the girl with the champagne, takes a glass, and begins to chat casually with a woman who approaches him, a simpering smile stretched across her face.

"Damn that girl," Evelyn says. "She never did bring me my vodka."

But I barely hear her. "Damien Stark," I say. My voice surprises me. It's little more than breath.

Evelyn's brows rise so high I notice the movement in my peripheral vision. "Well, how about that?" she says knowingly. "Looks like I guessed right."

"You did," I admit. "Mr. Stark is just the man I want to see."

I hope you enjoyed the excerpt! Grab your own copy of Release Me … or any of the books in the series now!

The Original Trilogy
Release Me

Claim Me

Complete Me

And Beyond...
Anchor Me

Lost With Me

Some rave reviews for J. Kenner's sizzling romances...

I just get sucked into these books and can not get enough of this series. They are so well written and as satisfying as each book is they leave you greedy for more. — Goodreads reviewer on *Wicked Torture*

A sizzling, intoxicating, sexy read!!!! J. Kenner had me devouring Wicked Dirty, the second installment of *Stark World Series* in one sitting. I loved everything about this book from the opening pages to the raw and vulnerable characters. With her sophisticated prose, Kenner created a love story that had the perfect blend of lust, passion, sexual tension, raw emotions and love. - Michelle, Four Chicks Flipping Pages

Wicked Dirty CLAIMED and CONSUMED every ounce of me from the very first page. Mind racing. Pulse pounding. Breaths bated. Feels flowing. Eyes wide in anticipation. Heart beating out of my chest. I felt the current of *Wicked Dirty* flow through me. I was DRUNK on this book that was my fine whiskey, so smooth and spectacular, and could not get enough of this *Wicked Dirty* drink. - Karen Bookalicious Babes Blog

"Sinfully sexy and full of heart. Kenner shines in this second chance, slow burn of a romance. Wicked Grind is the perfect book to kick off your summer."- *K. Bromberg, New York Times bestselling author (on Wicked Grind)*

"J. Kenner never disappoints~her books just get better and better." - *Mom's Guilty Pleasure (on Wicked Grind)*

"I don't think J. Kenner could write a bad story if she tried. ... Wicked Grind is a great beginning to what I'm positive will be a very successful series. ... The line forms here." *iScream Books (On Wicked Grind)*

"Scorching, sweet, and soul-searing, *Anchor Me* is the ultimate love story that stands the test of time and tribulation. THE TRUEST LOVE!" *Bookalicious Babes Blog (on Anchor Me)*

"J. Kenner has brought this couple to life and the character connection that I have to these two holds no bounds and that is testament to J.

Kenner's writing ability." *The Romance Cover (on Anchor Me)*

"J. Kenner writes an emotional and personal story line. … The premise will captivate your imagination; the characters will break your heart; the romance continues to push the envelope." *The Reading Café (on Anchor Me)*

"Kenner may very well have cornered the market on sinfully attractive, dominant antiheroes and the women who swoon for them . . ." *Romantic Times*

"*Wanted* is another J. Kenner masterpiece . . . This was an intriguing look at self-discovery and forbidden love all wrapped into a neat little action-suspense package. There was plenty of sexual tension and eventually action. Evan was hot, hot, hot! Together, they were combustible. But can we expect anything less from J. Kenner?" *Reading Haven*

"*Wanted* by J. Kenner is the whole package! A toe-curling smokin' hot read, full of incredible characters and a brilliant storyline that you won't be able to get enough of. I can't wait for the next book in this series . . . I'm hooked!" *Flirty & Dirty Book Blog*

"J. Kenner's evocative writing thrillingly captures the power of physical attraction, the pull of long-ing, the universe-altering effect one person can have on another. . . . *Claim Me* has the emotional depth to back up the sex . . . Every scene is infused with both erotic tension, and the tension of wondering what lies beneath Damien's veneer – and how and when it will be revealed." *Heroes and Heartbreakers*

"*Claim Me* by J. Kenner is an erotic, sexy and exciting ride. The story between Damien and Nikki is amazing and written beautifully. The intimate and detailed sex scenes will leave you fanning your-self to cool down. With the writing style of Ms. Kenner you almost feel like you are there in the story riding along the emotional rollercoaster with Damien and Nikki." *Fresh Fiction*

"PERFECT for fans of *Fifty Shades of Grey* and *Bared to You*. *Release Me* is a powerful and erotic romance novel that is sure to make adult romance readers sweat, sigh and swoon." *Reading, Eating & Dreaming Blog*

"I will admit, I am in the 'I loved *Fifty Shades*' camp,

but after reading *Release Me*, Mr. Grey only scratches the surface compared to Damien Stark." *Cocktails and Books Blog*

"It is not often when a book is so amazingly well-written that I find it hard to even begin to accurately describe it . . . I recommend this book to everyone who is interested in a passionate love story." *Romancebookworm's Reviews*

"The story is one that will rank up with the *Fifty Shades* and Cross Fire trilogies." *Incubus Publishing Blog*

"The plot is complex, the characters engaging, and J. Kenner's passionate writing brings it all perfectly together." *Harlequin Junkie*

Seduce Me

Unwrap Me

Deepest Kiss

Entice Me

Hold Me

Please Me

The Steele Books/Stark International:

He was the only man who made her feel alive.

Say My Name

On My Knees

Under My Skin

Take My Dare (includes short story Steal My Heart)

Stark International Novellas:

Meet Jamie & Ryan-so hot it sizzles.

Tame Me

Tempt Me

S.I.N. Trilogy:

It was wrong for them to be together…

…but harder to stay apart.

Dirtiest Secret

Hottest Mess

Sweetest Taboo

Stand alone novels:

Most Wanted:

Three powerful, dangerous men.

Three sensual, seductive women.

Wanted

Heated

Ignited

Wicked Nights (Stark World):

Sometimes it feels so damn good to be bad.

Wicked Grind

Wicked Dirty

Wicked Torture

Man of the Month

Who's your man of the month …?

Down On Me

Hold On Tight

Need You Now

Start Me Up

Get It On

In Your Eyes

Turn Me On

Shake It Up

All Night Long

In Too Deep

Light My Fire

Walk The Line

Bar Bites: A Man of the Month Cookbook(by J. Kenner & Suzanne M. Johnson)

Additional Titles

Wild Thing

One Night (A Stark World short story in the Second Chances anthology)

Also by Julie Kenner

The Protector (Superhero) Series:
The Cat's Fancy (prequel)
Aphrodite's Kiss
Aphrodite's Passion
Aphrodite's Secret
Aphrodite's Flame
Aphrodite's Embrace (novella)
Aphrodite's Delight (novella – free download)

Demon Hunting Soccer Mom Series:
Carpe Demon
California Demon
Demons Are Forever
Deja Demon
The Demon You Know (short story)
Demon Ex Machina

Also by Julie Kenner

Pax Demonica
Day of the Demon

The Dark Pleasures Series:
Caress of Darkness
Find Me In Darkness
Find Me In Pleasure
Find Me In Passion
Caress of Pleasure

The Blood Lily Chronicles:
Tainted
Torn
Turned

Rising Storm:
Rising Storm: Tempest Rising
Rising Storm: Quiet Storm

Devil May Care:
Seducing Sin
Tempting Fate

About the Author

J. Kenner (aka Julie Kenner) is the *New York Times*, *USA Today*, *Publishers Weekly*, *Wall Street Journal* and #1 International bestselling author of over eighty novels, novellas and short stories in a variety of genres.

JK has been praised by *Publishers Weekly* as an author with a "flair for dialogue and eccentric characterizations" and by *RT Bookclub* for having "cornered the market on sinfully attractive, dominant antiheroes and the women who swoon for them." A five-time finalist for Romance Writers of America's prestigious RITA award, JK took home the first RITA trophy awarded in the category of erotic romance in 2014 for her novel, *Claim Me* (book 2 of her Stark Trilogy).

In her previous career as an attorney, JK worked as a lawyer in Southern California and Texas. She currently lives in Central Texas, with her husband, two daughters, and two rather spastic cats.

More ways to connect:

www.jkenner.com

Text JKenner to 21000 for JK's text alerts.

 facebook.com/jkennerbooks

twitter.com/juliekenner